BLADE'S DE:

Desire, Oklahoma 2

Leah Brooke

EROTIC ROMANCE

Siren Publishing, Inc.
www.SirenPublishing.com

A SIREN PUBLISHING BOOK
IMPRINT: Erotic Romance

BLADE'S DESIRE
Copyright © 2009 by Leah Brooke

ISBN-10: 1-60601-286-X
ISBN-13: 978-1-60601-286-4

First Publication: June 2009

Cover design by Jinger Heaston
All cover art and logo copyright © 2009 by Siren Publishing, Inc.

PUBLISHER
Siren Publishing, Inc.
www.SirenPublishing.com

DEDICATION

To my family for their encouragement and patience.
I could never do this without you.

Special thanks to my mother for her support
and for always believing in me.

BLADE'S DESIRE

Desire, Oklahoma 2

LEAH BROOKE
Copyright © 2009

Chapter One

Kelly Jones finally finished unpacking the supplies that had arrived earlier that day. She and Jesse Erickson, her best friend and business partner, had been so busy with customers that neither had had a chance to unpack until now.

Their business, *Indulgences,* kept them very busy on Fridays and Saturdays. Today, a hot and humid Friday, had been no exception. Since opening almost two months ago, their customer base had grown so fast that both Kelly and Jesse had almost worn themselves out trying to keep up with it.

It had taken Kelly and Jesse's two husbands, Clay and Rio, to convince Jesse that the store needed to hire more help. With the store closed Sundays and Mondays and the high school girls they'd hired working nights and Saturdays, it had become a lot less stressful.

"Whew! Well, I closed up out front. Business is really picking up." Jesse smiled at Kelly as she eyed the packages on the table. "Did we get everything we ordered?"

"Yes, all of it." Kelly nodded and gestured to the assortment of herbs and scented oils she hadn't yet put away. "I want to start experimenting with scents next week." She started putting the items in one of the overflowing cabinets. "I can't wait until we get the new cabinets installed. It's so hard to find anything."

They wanted to branch out into a men's line and Kelly couldn't wait to get started. She closed her eyes. If she could find a way to duplicate Blade's clean, earthy scent, they could make a fortune.

"Yeah, I know what you mean. And with adding all these new ingredients, it's going to be even harder to find anything," Jesse agreed and turned to Frank Elliott. Frank had just recently been hired after Clay and Rio found him in a ditch, badly beaten.

"Thanks for getting rid of the boxes, Frank. As soon as you take them out, you go ahead to Miss Gracie's."

Frank frowned and looked at Jesse. "But Mr. Clay and Mr. Rio said not to leave you alone."

He did whatever Jesse and Kelly asked of him, without hesitation, except when it conflicted with Clay and Rio's wishes.

"It's okay." Jesse guided Frank toward the back door. "I promise we'll be leaving in a few minutes. You tell Miss Gracie that I need a dozen orders of chicken and dumplings and two apple pies to go. I'll be there in a few minutes to pick them up. I just want to talk to Miss Kelly a minute."

Frank still looked worried, but reluctantly left.

"You know he's going to call them," Kelly smiled as she resumed her task. "A dozen orders and two pies?"

"You've seen them all eat. I threw myself on Gracie's mercy long ago. I want to talk to you."

Kelly continued to put things away, aware of Jesse's scrutiny.

Jesse leaned against the counter and crossed her arms over her chest. "How are things with you and Blade?"

Kelly shrugged. "What do you mean?"

"I think you know." Jesse's eyes were sharp. "Ever since we moved here, he's been sniffing around you. He's been watching you since that first day, when you and Cullen got here in the moving van."

Cullen, Kelly's older brother, had been visiting her while Jesse visited her sister, Nat, here in Desire. When Jesse called Kelly, asking her to move here, Kelly, wanting to escape Simon, an abusive ex boyfriend who kept coming around, had jumped at the chance.

Blade's dark good looks and fierce scrutiny had made Kelly edgy from the beginning. A man of few words, Blade hid his thoughts behind a cool mask and amused gaze.

The intensity with which he regarded her had terrified her at first. The only times she'd ever been on the receiving end of such attention in the past was when she was about to be beaten and raped by Simon.

Kelly had learned to avoid Blade like the plague.

Little by little, the fear she'd felt around him had changed to something else, an awareness she fought to overlook.

"Kelly?"

Kelly lifted her eyes and saw that Jesse watched her knowingly.

"Kelly, I know what you've been through," Jesse murmured softly. She reached out to touch Kelly's shoulder.

"I think you're ready, Kelly. Don't keep putting distance between yourself and Blade. Give yourself and him a chance. Don't let what Simon did to you keep you alone for the rest of your life."

"I'm scared," Kelly admitted softly. She looked down at the fragrant herbs in her hands. "You know the kind of man Blade is, Jesse. He's a Dom! He and his partners train other Doms. What if it doesn't work? I don't want to feel helpless ever again. What if I can't let go of my fear during sex? You know that Blade would want me to submit. Being with a Dom would make me feel helpless again."

Jesse hugged her friend. "Does Nat seem helpless to you?"

Kelly smiled reluctantly. Jesse's sister had been married to a Dom for years. Kelly had no idea what went on in their bedroom, of course, but out of it, Jake and Nat's love and devotion to each other showed clearly. Jake utterly adored his mischievous wife and Nat glowed with happiness.

"They're in love, Jesse." Kelly sighed. "It makes all the difference in the world."

"If Blade isn't in love with you, Kelly, I'll eat Clay and Rio's hats, dust and all." Jesse smiled. "He's a good man, Kelly. I asked Clay and Rio about him. They say they've never met a man with more patience than Blade."

Jesse waited until Kelly's eyes met hers. "He's been patient with you, hasn't he?"

Kelly thought about Blade's non-threatening touches and how carefully he treated her. They'd known each other for two months, had been together almost every day and he hadn't even kissed her yet.

"Yes," Kelly nodded reluctantly. "Blade has been very patient with me."

"You're crazy about him, aren't you?"

"I'm not sure what I feel." Kelly shook her head. "Thinking about Blade touching me scares me to death. Thinking about him touching another woman makes me feel like hitting something."

Kelly nervously began to pace the workroom. "Blade will always touch other women, Jesse. His job demands it. How would you feel if Clay or Rio were constantly around naked women eager to please them, touching them to train other men in how to get them to respond?"

Kelly watched her friend grimace. "You have a point. But, you know he doesn't have sex with them, right? Rio told me that Blade, Royce, and King never had sex on the job. And we both know what kinds of things go on at the club. Don't you think Clay, Rio, and Jake are there watching when some of the other men fuck a woman in the main room? Do you think they join in?"

Jesse gathered her purse. "Don't make the mistake I almost made. If it wasn't for Nat, I never would have gotten involved with Clay and Rio."

Kelly watched Jesse walk to the door and turn back, startled at the tears glistening in Jesse's eyes.

"Look what I would have missed. Please give it a chance, Kelly. Believe me, it's worth it."

Kelly stood staring at the door as it closed behind Jesse. Did she have the courage to follow her friend's advice?"

Absently, she locked up downstairs and went up to her apartment. As soon as she reached her bedroom, she began stripping off clothes, anxious for a hot shower.

Standing under the spray, she thought about what Jesse had said. Closing her eyes, she pictured Blade. She longed to be able to free the shoulder length black hair Blade kept tied back. Thinking about the way those piercing dark blue eyes looked at her hardened her nipples and made her stomach clench.

Little tingles of awareness shot through her and she covered her breasts with her hands, imagining that Blade touched her. Moving her hand down her body, over her stomach, then lower, Kelly pressed her fingers against her aching clit. Rubbing gently, then more furiously, Kelly sobbed. She couldn't find the release she craved. Frustrated, she pinched her nipple as she fought to orgasm.

Her sobs became worse and she doubled her efforts, but release escaped her. Finally admitting defeat, Kelly slumped to the shower floor, crying softly. She couldn't even pleasure herself.

Without ever experiencing his touch, her body nevertheless knew its master. Kelly knew Blade would be the only one who could give her the pleasure and release her body demanded. He started this fire and it appeared that only he could put it out.

Never having had an orgasm, Kelly could only imagine how it would feel. She'd been a virgin when she met Simon and when he took her, he had only his own pleasure in mind. When sex turned to beatings and rape, what little enjoyment Kelly had felt turned to fear and pain.

She wanted to feel it. She needed to know the pleasure to be found between a man and a woman. Her body would no longer be denied.

The more time she spent with Blade, the more aware she became of her body's response to him. That tingle of awareness whenever she saw him became stronger and stronger. Now she felt a sharp jolt every time he got close to her, one that shot straight through her, making her nipples hard and sensitive and her pussy weep.

Her body reacted to Blade as it reacted to no one else.

Standing, she turned off the shower and got out, briskly drying her over sensitive body, and donning her robe. Sitting on the edge of her bed, she absently began to run a comb through her hair. What could she do?

It was apparent that Blade waited for something. Maybe for her to make the first move?

Could she do it? Could she go to Blade and tell him that she might be ready for a physical relationship?

What if he didn't want her that way?

No. Remembering the times he'd let her see the desire in his eyes, Kelly knew that he wanted her.

But, did he really care for her?

Standing, she began to pace her bedroom. He had to care at least a little for her to be as patient as he'd been. Two months and he hadn't so much as kissed her!

What could she say to him?

'Hey Blade. I'm ready for our relationship to become physical.'

No. That would never do. What if he said, 'What relationship? We're just friends.'

No. She couldn't say that.

She couldn't even be sure she would be able to submit to him the way she knew he'd demand.

Wait. There always seemed to be women there. They had to be training the women how to learn to surrender control to their Doms. As much as they trained the Doms, wouldn't the women have to be trained, too?

What if she asked Blade to help her the way he'd probably already helped countless other women? She could tell him her fears of being helpless, unable to fight a man's strength when she felt the most vulnerable.

She would be able to find out not only if she could have sex again, but if she could enjoy a physical relationship with Blade, a man who would dominate in the bedroom even more than other men.

And, she could do it without Blade ever knowing she'd fallen in love with him.

If she found out she couldn't handle being submissive to Blade's dominance, she wouldn't have the added embarrassment of having him shun her feelings if he didn't feel the same.

Yes, it might be the perfect solution.

If Blade cared for her and she could handle sex with him, it would all work out. If not, well, at least she'd tried and would learn something about herself, even if she discovered that she could only enjoy straight sex, or if she could even enjoy sex at all.

Moving to her closet, she jerked a sundress from its hangar. She would go to Blade now, before she lost her nerve.

Chapter Two

Blade Royal leaned back in his leather chair and rubbed his eyes. A glance at his watch told him he had been in the club's online chat room for over four hours.

The online chat room was a service the club provided, for a significant fee, to the club's long distance members who wanted advice, support, or to share information and experiences regarding the dominate lifestyle.

Some of the men, confused about their need to dominate, got support and help with understanding this need.

Some wanted advice on the best ways to use the toys available to give a woman the ultimate pleasure.

Others, like the one Blade had been trying to deal with for the last several hours, seemed hell bent on using their dominate natures as an excuse to hurt or abuse women.

He typed in yet another response, wondering what it would take to get through to this so called Dominant.

I've told you, hurting your submissive is not the point. Erotic pain ONLY!

The thought that this man bullied and hurt women, excusing his behavior by claiming to be a Dom infuriated him. He'd love to be able to cut this guy off but couldn't give up the opportunity to try to get through to him.

But I thought a Dominant's main goal is to make a woman beg. You said that yourself. I've learned that pain makes a woman beg real good.

Blade couldn't help but wonder how many times Kelly had begged for the beatings, the rapes, the pain to stop.

A Dom wants his submissive to beg for release. Not beg for the pain to stop! Your goal is to give her the ultimate pleasure, pleasure she can find only with you.

So what's the point in having whips and clamps and plugs to shove up their asses if you can't use them?

Blade ran a hand tiredly over his face. In the hands of an experienced and patient Dom, these items could give a submissive great pleasure. He would use such things on Kelly, making her feel nothing but pleasure as she came, screaming his name.

You can use them if you use them safely to give your submissive EROTIC pain and pleasure. Your pleasure will come from making her so aroused she will let you do anything you want to her. She will beg you to take her however you want. You must control her with her own pleasure. Only then will you be in charge.

How am I supposed to know what they want? They all want something different. I'm in charge a lot faster if they're in pain!

Blade's fists clenched in fury. He wondered if that's what Simon, Kelly's abusive ex boyfriend had thought.

Don't hurt them! Any pain should give pleasure and should not be cruel or excessive. You must pay attention! It takes time, patience and understanding. Be patient and watch your sub closely as she adjusts to each new experience. Pay close attention to her reaction. You must not miss even the slightest nuance of her response.

Blade couldn't wait to begin with Kelly. He loved a challenge. Kelly wouldn't be mastered, but what a challenge to try. He couldn't wait to start teaching her just how much passion lurked inside that voluptuous little body. First, though, he had to get her to trust him.

How am I supposed to get off if I'm too busy paying attention to her?

Blade sighed and rubbed the back of his neck in exasperation. Why didn't this guy just do everyone a favor and masturbate?

You need to be patient. Take the time to get to know your sub well. Your pleasure will be much greater if she's so aroused she wants release more than she wants her next breath.

The bitch I fuck used to like it when I beat her pussy. I did it to her all the time, just like she wanted. Now she doesn't want it anymore. How the hell am I supposed to know what they want if they can't make up their fucking minds?

Predictable asshole. No fucking imagination at all.

You must keep everything fresh. You have to keep her guessing. Don't become predictable. Predictable is boring. Practice arousing her with only words. A good Dom can get a woman very aroused using only words.

"I can only imagine the conversations you have with your subs. Maybe talking will keep you out of trouble or at least let them know what they're in for," Blade muttered to himself.

So do you think I should get a new sub?

Blade grimaced, muttering to himself again. "I think you should get an inflatable doll."

You should spend time learning your woman. Delay your pleasure. You have to see to hers. Once you can control hers, you'll be in charge.

How the fuck can I be in charge if she gets all the pleasure?

"Why do I feel like I'm beating my head against a fucking wall?"

A Dom controls a submissive with her own pleasure!!! You can never be in charge unless you learn how to give her pleasure greater than she has ever known. Then you must teach her how to delay her pleasure. You will have to do it for her at first. Learn the signs of her impending release, then you can keep her on the edge without letting her go over. But not for too long. When she does have an orgasm, the delay will make it that much stronger.

The bitches I fuck all want to come right away. I'll have to get a new one. I found one cunt I want. She's not a sub, NOT YET. I know I can dominate her. Snooty bitch! She doesn't want anything to do with me. YET. But I'm going to teach her how to be a good little sub.

Fuck! He hoped like hell this woman continued to avoid this asshole. He had to get through to him.

No! You cannot take a woman against her will! That's RAPE! She must be a consenting adult.

His jaw clenched, remembering the rage he'd felt when he'd learned about Kelly's beatings and rapes. He'd do whatever he could to make sure it didn't happen to another woman.

I'm not going to rape anybody. She wants it. I have to go to work now. Bye.

Blade leaned back and sighed when Master X signed off. He closed his eyes tiredly, wondering if anything he'd said had penetrated.

The thought of this guy hurting these women infuriated him. He could only hope he didn't do to them what had been done to Kelly.

Kelly had lost the ability to trust. It had taken him weeks to earn just a small amount, which he treasured. With time and patience, he knew he could earn more.

Another glance at his watch told him that she would be done working for the day. The store she and Jesse owned had been closed for nearly an hour.

The time had finally come to show Kelly exactly how good things could be between them. He knew she would make the perfect sub for him and he couldn't wait to get started. He would keep her so satisfied that she would never think of sex any other way ever again.

Anxious to put his plan into action, he pushed back from his massive wood desk and started for the door. When the intercom on his desk sounded, he bit back his annoyance.

He took two long strides and jabbed the button.

"Yes, Sebastian?"

"Master Blade, there is a Kelly Jones here to see you."

Kelly had managed to do something few ever did. She'd taken him by surprise.

Leaning back against his desk, he wondered what had brought her here when she'd never come before. Thoughts of her ex boyfriend coming to town flitted through his mind.

"Where is she?"

Sebastian's cool voice with a slight French accent came through the intercom. "I escorted her to the private sitting room."

"I'll be right down."

Kelly clasped her hands on her knees when they trembled so badly they knocked together.

Why had she come here? Had she lost her mind?

When she'd arrived, the very formal butler had shown no surprise at finding a woman on the doorstep. He'd shown her to this room as though women appeared at the door every day.

Oh God! She could *not* do this. She had to do this. If he'd taught other women how to give up control, he could teach her.

Isn't that why she was here after all? To be one of these women?

Kelly jumped up. How many women came here for the same reason? How many of them had Blade touched? How many of them had he fucked? Would she become just another in a long line?

She raced to the doorway, cursing the heels she'd worn. She had to get out of here! There had to be another way to do this.

Kelly froze in her tracks when Blade's shoulders filled the doorway.

"Going somewhere, love?"

Kelly felt her nipples tighten. She crossed her arms over her chest, hoping she looked nonchalant as she attempted to hide it. Blade had never used an endearment with her before and certainly had never used that tone of voice.

The look in his eyes shocked her into immobility. Possessive fire shot from his dark eyes as he looked at her in a way he never had before. They glittered with emotion, one she didn't have the time to discern before he shuttered them, allowing her to see only the gentle amusement he usually showed her.

Kelly could hear her own harsh breathing in the heavy silence. She swallowed painfully, trying to calm her racing heart as Blade closed the door behind him and stood with his arms crossed over his chest, mocking her stance.

He raised a brow at her continued silence and it took several long seconds before she remembered he'd asked her a question.

"I, um, I wanted to um. I'd better go." Kelly walked hesitantly toward the doorway, knowing she'd have to get past Blade to leave. Instead of stepping aside, he moved toward her, grasped her elbow, and turned her back into the room.

Panicked, she tried to pull away. Blade merely tightened his hold and led her back to the overstuffed chair she'd recently vacated. He moved to a leather chair a few feet away, which he angled to face hers.

Kelly started to scoot forward. She shouldn't have come. Why didn't she think about this a little more before she left home? She had to get out of here.

"If you move from that chair, I'll take it as an invitation to paddle your bottom."

Kelly felt her eyes widen and her heart gallop as though it would burst through her chest. Her nipples tightened painfully and she felt an unbelievable rush of moisture between her thighs. Had she ever felt like this before? If so, she didn't remember.

Did he just threaten to spank her? And why did the thought of that excite her? She'd been hit many times and it had never excited her.

She knew her eyes widened as she stared at him. This was a far different Blade than she'd dealt with before. Oh, he had the same dark good looks, the same dark blue eyes, and lean muscular frame.

A darker Blade shone through, as if a veil had been lifted. She'd always known him as patient and gentle, but always with good-natured amusement in his eyes. And though he watched and waited patiently for her as though giving her time to settle, she saw a sharpness to his gaze that had never been directed at her before.

Kelly lowered her eyes and wiped her sweaty palms over her shaky knees, smoothing the material of her sundress nervously. When he spoke, she glanced up from beneath lowered lashes.

"Not that I'm not delighted that you've come to visit me, love, but you've never done it before. May I ask why you've suddenly decided to do so now?"

His voice definitely sounded different. The intense way he watched her made her jittery. To her amazement and horror, it also made her pussy clench and weep. She'd never felt a need like this before.

Being around Blade usually filled her with an increasing awareness, but this Blade affected her more, much more.

She stared at him, mesmerized by the look in his eyes. When he lifted an elegant brow, she realized he once again waited for an answer.

Kelly cleared her throat and struggled to come up with something to say. Facing the intensity of Blade's dominance had her rethinking her plan.

"I just, um, wanted to see you." Kelly smiled tremulously at Blade's continued perusal. "I thought we could have dinner."

Several long seconds passed. Blade watched Kelly squirm as he regarded her intently and wondered if she really thought she would get away with lying to him. He blamed himself. He'd allowed her to get away with a lot because he knew she worked hard to recover from an abusive relationship and he hadn't wanted to spook her.

But she'd come as far as she could on her own. The time had come for him to pick up the reins and claim his woman.

"Lying to me has my hand itching to make your bottom so red you won't be able to sit down for dinner. Last chance, love. Why are you here?"

Blade watched his beloved turn bright red and lower her eyes. He allowed her to get away with it for now, sensing she needed to hide to talk to him. She would soon learn that even that amount of hiding herself from him would not be tolerated.

"I need your help."

Her whisper barely sounded even in the quiet room. Her hands trembled as she alternately bunched and smoothed the hem of her sundress.

She looked lush and delicious in the blue dress, her curvy figure shown to perfection. He couldn't wait to see the color of the nipples poking at the cups of her dress or how her luscious ass would fit in his hands when he slid his cock into her.

He sat back in his chair trying to appear relaxed. He really wanted to rip that pretty blue dress off of her. Shifting in his seat, he hid a grimace, no longer surprised by the inevitable tightening in his groin around her.

Blade, known for his formidable control, felt that tight rein slip with her. Realizing he loved her had shaken him. Waiting for her to be ready for a physical relationship with him had stretched his nerves to the breaking point.

He would take care of whatever problem had brought her here. Then, he could finally concentrate on seducing her and showing her the pleasure he could give her as he taught her the pleasure of giving up control.

"What do you need my help with, love?" Remembering his earlier thought he frowned. "Simon hasn't contacted you, has he?"

"No, no, nothing like that."

Kelly knew she hadn't handled this well, but this more *potent* Blade made her so nervous and aroused she had a hard time keeping her thoughts together. The confidence she'd felt before Blade walked into the room vanished and she knew she acted like an idiot.

She closed her eyes and took several deep calming breaths, aware that Blade watched her and waited for an answer.

"I think I'm ready to, um, for physical intimacy again," she blurted before she lost her nerve.

"Yes, you are." Blade nodded calmly. "And?"

Jeez, he wanted her to say it. Kelly shifted, uncomfortably aware of her body's response to Blade's continued scrutiny.

"I've heard that you, um, accept women as clients to help them, um, with whatever you help them with." She waved her hand dismissively. "I want to hire you."

Thinking about Blade's dominant nature and her ability to be with him the way he would demand, she added, "I want to know if I could enjoy sex again and if I could learn to give up control in the bedroom."

For several long moments, silence filled the room. Kelly lowered her eyes, her gaze inadvertently coming to rest on his groin. The bulge she saw there only made her more nervous.

She may just need to reconsider this. She'd been prepared to face the Blade she knew, not this more…intense version. She had a feeling he would be even more overwhelming once they were in the bedroom. Lowering her eyes to rest on the hands fisted on her lap, she closed them, not at all certain she could handle this.

"Look at me, Kelly."

Kelly looked up without thinking, automatically reacting to the steely command in the softly spoken words.

"We do not take women as clients. Ever."

"But I thought -"

"We do, however, help women understand and learn the pleasures of being submissive. They are here when we train Doms. It's an education for all involved."

Kelly started to jump out of her seat. Remembering Blade's threat, she eyed him cautiously and sat back down.

"So, the women are touched by the Doms you're training?"

"Yes, along with Royce, King and I."

His mouth curved. "When the day's training is over, some also go down to the club room and enjoy being the center of attention with our members."

Kelly could feel the blood drain from her face. She knew she'd never be able to let all those people touch her. The thought of a bunch of strangers having their hands on her naked body filled her with revulsion and fear.

She shook her head. "I can't do that. I can't let all those people see me naked, touch me."

She looked at Blade pleadingly. "Isn't there another way? I don't want the club members to see me naked. Most of them live here, For God's sake! They're my neighbors!"

She took a deep breath. "I don't want to be touched by the Doms you're training either. I can't do that. I just can't. Can't you do it? I mean, I know you. I was hoping it would be you that, you know?"

Kelly forced herself to remain still as Blade studied her through hooded eyes. She had no idea of the thoughts going through his mind. She shifted restlessly, not sure if she'd offended him. Although they'd spent quite a bit of time together in the last several weeks, she didn't know him intimately enough to be able to read him.

It made her nervous. She'd learned early to read Simon. Knowing his moods had saved her more than once from being beaten and raped.

She watched as Blade tapped his finger against his chin thoughtfully.

"Let me see if I understand what you want from me."

Kelly held her breath as Blade continued.

"You want me to try to fuck you, to see if you would be able to go through with it?"

Kelly swallowed nervously. Why did it sound so awful when he said it? She shook her head at her own stupidity.

"No, no, it's not like that." Keeping her head lowered, she glanced at him nervously.

"I *want* to be with you." Suddenly shy, she licked her lips. She had to make him help her. "I'm just afraid, and you've always been very patient with me."

When he said nothing, Kelly looked up at him pleadingly. "Don't you understand? I want to have sex, but I'm afraid I won't be able to let go. You're a Dom. You know how to help me do it."

At Blade's continued silence, Kelly felt her eyes fill with tears.

"Damn it, Blade. I'm tired of letting what Simon did to me ruin my life. I want to live again. I want to be able to have sex again. Please, will you help me?"

Kelly's heart skipped a beat when Blade stood and loomed over her. Kelly automatically leaned back in her chair. Her nipples tightened painfully as her stomach clenched.

Blade caged her in by bracing himself with a hand on each of the arms of her chair. His eyes held hers, making her feel as though he could see into her soul. They burned with a knowledge she didn't understand.

Nothing could have prepared her for what he said next.

"For the next six weeks, you will do whatever I tell you to do. You will wear what I tell you to wear and all of your free time belongs to me.

"I will teach you how to trust me in all things. You will have no control in what I do to you. You will do what I tell you to do without question or hesitation. If you hesitate or question me, you will be subject to punishment in any way I see fit."

Kelly felt goosebumps break out all over.

"You will trust that I know what you are capable of tolerating, concerning both pleasure and pain. You will answer every question I ask truthfully and immediately."

Kelly felt her eyes widen. She'd never heard Blade talk like this before. No wonder men came to learn from him.

What had she gotten herself into? Her body hummed, aroused beyond belief, even as she shook, thinking about what he might have in store for her.

His touch since entering the room had been completely impersonal. He seduced her only with his words. How would her body react once his touch became more intimate?

"The only way to stop whatever you feel you can't handle," he continued in that same tone, "would be for you to say the words 'red light.'"

Kelly watched as Blade straightened and moved several feet away from her, hands on his hips.

"If you say those words, it stops everything."

When Kelly frowned, Blade nodded.

"Everything, Kelly. Without trust, we have nothing. We won't be anything more than two people living in the same town. Do you accept these terms?"

Kelly felt her stomach drop. She found herself neatly cornered. If she walked away now, she would never know if she and Blade had a chance.

She loved him.

She trusted him as she hadn't ever trusted another man. Could she trust him enough to be as vulnerable as a woman could be with a man?

Kelly only knew that for the rest of her life she would regret not taking this chance.

She also had to come to terms with the fact that if she accepted, there would be no turning back.

"What happens after six weeks?" Kelly asked cautiously.

"In six weeks our agreement is over. By that time, you will understand yourself better than you ever have. In many ways. After that, we'll talk again."

At her continued silence, he raised a brow. "Do you accept my terms?"

She could do this. She *had* to do this. She had six weeks with Blade, six weeks to see if she could be the kind of lover he would need. Six weeks from now, she would have the answers she needed to get on with her life.

"Can I ask you something?" Kelly shifted uncomfortably.

"Of course, love." His eyes were gentle, though still hot.

"Will there be any other women, I mean, um, I know you train Doms and..."

"I will not be fucking anyone but you for the next six weeks. And if you think about letting anyone else touch you, you'd better think again."

Kelly took a deep breath and folded her hands on her lap.

"Then I accept your terms."

Blade kept his face blank, careful not to let his relief show. He didn't fuck the subs who came to the club, even the ones who came with their Doms who shared.

He, Royce, and King didn't fuck woman indiscriminately. They had sex, sure, but only with the women they truly wanted to have sex with.

Blade hadn't had sex with another woman since the day Jesse's ex husband attacked Kelly and Jesse. Seeing Kelly hurt had enraged him. Seeing her try to help her friend while injured had awakened something in him he hadn't known existed.

Weeks later he realized he loved her. Since then, it had taken time and patience to get close to her. Her fear of men still showed.

Congratulating himself on each small victory as she let her guard down with him more and more, Blade struggled not to show the supreme satisfaction he'd felt the first time he'd aroused her.

Each day after that he'd pushed her further, increasing the height of her arousal each chance he got, utilizing years of experience and knowledge of a woman's body to his advantage.

He'd just decided that the woman he wanted to claim as his own was finally ready for him to begin her education and she showed up here, handing him the opportunity on a silver platter.

He now had six weeks of total control and exclusive access to Kelly's body. He couldn't have asked for more. By the end of the six weeks, he'd have her right where he wanted her.

He'd go slowly with her. He would slow his pace, knowing that's what Kelly needed. By the end of six weeks, she will have forgotten all about her abusive ex boyfriend.

Then, he would claim her.

But first he had to find out all that Simon had done to her. He needed to wipe all the past ugliness from her mind.

Moving a chair to sit directly in front of her, Blade lowered himself into it, and grasped her hands in his. He didn't want to miss anything.

"Look at me, Kelly."

When her eyes lifted, he began.

"How many men have you fucked?"

He ignored her wince at his blunt language. Shocking her would give him the truth. He planned to shock her a lot more in the near future.

"One."

"Your ex boyfriend, Simon was the only man who ever fucked you?"

"Yes."

When she tried to pull her hands from his, Blade merely tightened his grip, careful not to hurt her.

"Don't try to pull away from me. I have a few more questions."

The panic in her eyes pulled at him. He raised her hands to his lips, pressing his lips to her white knuckles.

"Easy, love. I just need to know a little more. It will help me to know what you need to enjoy sex again. You came to me because you trust me and know I can help you, remember?"

At her hesitant nod, he continued.

"Did you ever take him into your mouth?"

Blade ground his teeth together when she nodded as tears filled her eyes. "Why does that make you cry? Didn't you like it?"

Her whispered, "No," tugged at his heart.

"Didn't you want to?"

Kelly shook her head. "No, he, he made me."

"What else did he make you do?"

When she hesitated, he purposely sharpened his tone. "Answer me, Kelly, now. All of it."

When she tugged her hands out of his grasp, he allowed it, caging her in by leaning forward with an arm on each side of her.

"It's embarrassing," she murmured as she turned bright red.

Blade raised a brow.

"You're going to be a lot more embarrassed in a little while. Are you going to let it stop you from getting what you want?" He kept his features carefully schooled when her eyes widened and she shook her head. He hid a grin when she raised her chin defiantly.

"No. I'm not going to let anything get in the way. I'm not going to let what Simon did to me ruin my life."

"Good. Now, tell me what has been done to you. Everything."

When she hesitated, he growled menacingly.

"Now! Or you will find yourself over my knee and your bare ass will be redder than your face."

"He raped me. He hit me and raped me! Over and over! Everywhere. There. Is that what you wanted to know?"

It took all of Blade's control not to gather her into his arms. Tenderness would come later. When you lance a boil, you have to get all the poison out.

"He raped your pussy?"

"Yes."

"Your mouth?"

"Yes."

"Your ass?"

"Yes."

"Did you ever enjoy sex with him, maybe in the beginning?"

Blade could see her struggle for control, her sobs lessening with each breath.

"It was okay at first," she shrugged.

"Have you ever had an orgasm?"

"I don't know. I don't think so."

Blade watched her frown.

Obviously she hadn't. If she had, she certainly would have known it.

Blade pursed his lips thoughtfully and leaned back in his chair. He would have to tread carefully. The only sex Kelly had ever experienced had either been lackluster or brutal. She'd never known the pleasure her body could experience, unless…"

"Do you masturbate?"

"Yes. No. It doesn't work."

"Why not?"

"I never had those kinds of feeling until…."

"Until what?"

When Kelly ducked her head, he reached over and grasped her chin.

"Until what? Don't make me ask you the same question more than once, Kelly. I won't tolerate it again."

"Until I met you," she blurted.

Blade nodded in satisfaction. He'd known she'd begun to become aroused around him but didn't know if she'd admit it.

"Blade?"

"Yes, love?"

"Are we done with the questions?"

Blade could see her tremble. Her knuckles became white as she twisted her fingers together.

"For now. Why?"

"Well, what you, um, said before. That I would be even more embarrassed soon. Whatever it is, I wish you would do it before I lose my nerve. I'm really scared." She added the last as a whisper.

Blade folded his arms across his chest and regarded her thoughtfully. He hadn't been planning on beginning tonight, but seeing how nervous she'd become, he changed his mind. He would strip her and explore her body. Hopefully, it would make her a little less nervous next time. He would even bring her to orgasm, so she would have a taste of the pleasure he could give her.

"Never again think to tell me what to do to you or when."

He ignored her gasp and continued. "For the next six weeks you belong to me. I can do whatever I want to do to you, whenever I want to do it. If I want you to know what I'm going to do, I will tell you. You do not ask. Are we clear?"

Kelly's eyes looked huge in her flushed face and Blade held his breath.

When she nodded hesitantly, he let it out slowly, keeping his mask of control firmly in place. His arms itched to hold her.

He would get her mind off of Simon and his abuse. He didn't want that asshole between them. He had to get her to stop thinking about her past. He wanted her whole focus to be on him and her body. Filling her with need and anticipation would make her forget everything else.

Gently helping her from the chair, he turned to lead her from the room.

"Where are we going?"

When he raised a brow, she flushed.

"Sorry. I forgot."

"That's okay, love. I'll teach you to remember."

His lips twitched when she bit her lip anxiously.

"As for where we're going," with a hand at her back, he led her from the room. "We're going upstairs. You're going to strip and be restrained. It's time for me to inspect what now belongs to me."

Chapter Three

Kelly allowed Blade to lead her to the elevator, numb with disbelief. The numbness didn't last long enough. Soon, longing and fear threatened to bring her to her knees.

The firm command in Blade's voice made her tremble. With all she'd been through, how could the thought of being at Blade's mercy fill her with such *need*?

The hand at her waist felt hard and hot as he led her from the elevator and down a hallway. They passed several doors, finally stopping at one. She wondered briefly what lay behind all these closed doors. And did she really want to know?

"This is my personal playroom. Most of your training will take place in this room."

Kelly squeezed her eyes closed. *Oh, like that didn't sound ominous!*

Blade's warm breath on her ear made her shiver, the heat from his body searing her back and bottom.

"Your body will learn to anticipate the pleasure found through this door. Soon, just walking down this hallway will arouse you and you'll be wet with need before you ever cross the threshold."

Trembling, she started when he nipped her earlobe.

"Your body will learn who its master is. It will crave both pleasure and pain at my hand and you won't have any choice but to accept whatever I give you. Your own body will betray you."

Okay, Kelly you can do this.

Blade's hand smoothed over her bottom and she jolted.

"There will be punishment for any and all infractions, which you will accept without complaint. Are we clear?"

Nodding, she knew she would do anything to keep feeling as she did now. With Blade near, her body already screamed with need.

A sharp slap on her bottom had her eyes popping open. He stood beside her, frowning.

"Are. We. Clear?"

"Yes, Blade." Kelly hardly recognized her own voice. The heat on her bottom spread in a surprising way.

"Good."

Blade unlocked the door, then turned to usher her through it.

Standing just inside the room, Kelly's trembling increased when Blade closed the door behind them. She heard the click of the lock but couldn't take her eyes from the room they'd just entered.

Mirrors filled one wall. On the others she saw hooks and shelves holding what appeared to be a variety of erotic play toys.

She didn't have a clue what most of them could be used for.

A padded table in the center of the room, with cuffs and hooks attached all around it made her swallow nervously.

She could do this. She *had* to do this. She couldn't bear to think about the alternative. Even afraid, she could feel her arousal build. Her panties had become soaked and her nipples all but cried for attention. She knew that Blade could give her the relief her body craved.

"Take off your shoes."

Wiping her damp palms on her sundress, she slipped off her sandals. When she saw that Blade held his hand out, she picked them up and handed them to him.

"Now the dress."

Why didn't he kiss her or something? She'd thought he would be the one undressing her in the heat of passion. Now she would have to stand there and let him see her naked.

Hesitating, she looked at Blade from the corner of her eye. When he frowned, she shifted nervously.

"I'm a little fat."

"No, you're not. You're voluptuous. Holding a woman who's nothing but skin and bones has never appealed to me. You're perfect."

Her inner glow at his praise didn't last long as he continued.

"However, I will not tolerate hesitation in obeying my orders, nor will I put up with remarks about your weight. If I think you need to lose weight, I will tell you. Your body now belongs to me, and I will not allow you to criticize what's mine." Blade wagged his fingers impatiently. "I dislike repeating myself, Kelly."

Her hands shook with a combination of fear and excitement. Blade's commanding tone combined with the intense glitter in his eyes had her nipples pebbling even harder and soaking her panties even more. For the first time in her life, she felt a strange heaviness in her abdomen. Her clit also throbbed, a sensation completely unfamiliar and almost overwhelming.

Clumsy with nerves, Kelly unzipped her dress and lifted it over her head. She handed it to Blade, crossing her arms over her ample breasts. She hadn't been able to wear a bra with the dress.

"Hands at your sides!"

Kelly jumped at Blade's harsh command. She felt a sharp pull in her abdomen and tried to stay still as her pussy clenched helplessly.

Standing in front of Blade wearing only her panties, she couldn't help but feel extremely self conscious of her near nudity. She felt so frumpy next to his dark good looks.

When she lifted her eyes to his, she expected the disgust that had always been in Simon's. What she saw, though, heated her blood and kept her eyes locked on his. The way they glittered filled her with hunger that made her tremble and burn.

He looked like he wanted to eat her alive.

Her body reacted with a fire of its own. Her skin suddenly felt too hot and too tight for her body as he continued to stare at her for several long minutes.

She didn't know how much longer she could stand his perusal. Her bones felt as if they had turned to jelly and she had to lock her knees to keep her legs from collapsing.

"Now the panties. And don't try to hide your body from me again."

Fumbling, she pulled the scrap of lace down past her knees and carefully stepped out of it. She hesitantly handed her panties to Blade, embarrassed by their dampness. She flushed when Blade lifted them to his nose and inhaled deeply.

He closed his eyes as though savoring her scent before turning and placing all of her clothing on a bench against the wall behind him. When he turned back to her, she struggled to keep her arms at her sides. She wanted to cover herself, alarmed by the fierceness of his gaze.

Grasping her hand, he pulled her to the center of the room.

"Stay right here. I'm just going to get the cuffs. You will be restrained while I explore your body."

Oh, my God! Kelly reminded herself to breathe. She could feel the moisture on her thighs now. Why did his words excite her instead of scaring her to death?

The underlying steel in both Blade's voice and his eyes should have her screaming her safe word and running for her clothes. She feared losing control and being vulnerable. Didn't she?

She couldn't imagine doing this with anyone but Blade, though. With anyone else, she never would have made it through the door. She trusted him as she trusted no one else.

She loved him.

Hopefully, he wouldn't realize it during the next six weeks. If all went well, she would tell him after the six weeks had passed. If he found out before then, he would be angry that she had manipulated him into this. Or worse, pity her and extricate himself from their agreement.

She needed this time to be sure of herself before telling him. She needed to be sure she could be the kind of woman *he* needed.

She watched him warily as he gathered several items and returned to stand in front of her.

"You're beautiful, love."

Kelly flushed under his scrutiny.

"If that makes you blush, you're sure to be bright red long before I'm done," Blade chuckled. "Now be still while I attach these."

Kelly watched in fascination as Blade attached a cuff to each of her wrists. His eyes held hers as he lifted them above her head. Trembling, she heard a click and glanced up. He'd attached both of her wrists to a ring above her, which hung from the ceiling.

Attached to the ring, Kelly saw a thick nylon rope. As Blade pulled the rope it lifted the ring until her arms straightened over her head.

Kelly watched as he looked down at her breasts. When she followed his gaze, she flushed. Her breasts had now lifted to him as if in invitation, her nipples hard and pointed.

She closed her eyes to block the sight. She needed him to touch her breasts so badly, she ached.

"Please, Blade," she heard herself whimper.

"Please what?"

"Please touch me," she practically sobbed.

"Excuse me?"

Opening her eyes she saw Blade frowning at her. With his hands on his hips, he looked fierce and menacing and she wanted him to touch her more than she'd ever wanted anything in her life.

"I'm sorry. I can't help it. I want you to touch me so badly I can't stand it."

Blade's features softened. "I know, love. But you have to learn to wait. I'll touch you when and how I want to touch you. *You* don't decide. I do. Now be still, so I can get your legs secured."

Blade grasped her ankles and positioned her feet a little more than shoulder distance apart, expertly attaching her cuffs to rings on the floor. Her arms now stretched even more over her head but they didn't feel pulled.

He had positioned her so that she stood completely spread and open for him.

Watching him, Kelly squirmed helplessly, desperate for his touch. She jolted when he straightened and closed his hands over her wrists.

"Are these all right? Are they pulling too tightly?"

"No." Kelly shook her head. Her heart pounded in her chest, as her breath caught in her throat.

His quick grin flashed just before his mouth covered hers. She automatically tried to put her arms around his neck and groaned when she couldn't, belatedly remembering she couldn't move them.

Her whole being felt alive in sensation, burning for whatever he would do to her. His kiss, demanding and thorough, drew from her a response she hadn't known she could give.

When he lifted his mouth from hers and straightened, she moaned helplessly.

"Now it's time to inspect my property."

Kelly knew somewhere in the back of her mind that she should object his words, but forgot everything as he ran his hands slowly up and down her arms, making her shudder and tingle all over.

She ached. Oh God, she ached. Nothing had ever prepared her for longing like this.

Blade's hands moved to her shoulders and neck, stroking lightly as he touched every square millimeter of her skin.

"You are incredibly soft, incredibly responsive. I now absolutely love the scent of vanilla."

His fingers traced under her arms and chest before moving to her breasts. With no pattern to his movements as he learned her body, she couldn't anticipate his touch in any specific place.

She wanted it anywhere. Everywhere.

He avoided her nipples and Kelly whimpered and unconsciously arched, desperate to have them touched. Her eyes fluttered closed.

When Blade lifted his hands from her, Kelly's eyes popped open and she sobbed. "Please, no! Please touch me!"

Without a word, Blade reached out and pinched her nipples between his thumbs and forefingers. Hard.

Kelly froze.

Blade's hold on her nipples tightened more and more until Kelly whimpered. "It hurts. Oh God, please Blade. It hurts!"

Blade pinched harder and she gasped, unable to struggle, stretched out this way.

"You wanted me to touch your nipples, Kelly. Isn't that what you wanted?"

"No! It hurts! Please stop."

"Are you using your safe word?"

Kelly couldn't believe the pain, but she couldn't let Blade walk away from her.

"No!"

"Are you going to let me finish my exam? Are you going to be quiet or tell me again what you think you need?"

"I'll be quiet." Kelly gasped again at the tug on her nipples. "I'm yours. I'm sorry. I want you to finish. Touch me however you want. I'll be good. I promise."

With a last punishing twist, Blade released her throbbing nipples. The sharp sensation traveled straight to her pussy and clit and her knees gave out.

Blade caught her around the waist to steady her as the cuffs pulled at her wrists.

"Easy, love," he chuckled. "You're far more responsive than I thought you'd be this soon."

His eyes stayed steady, blazing hot as he regarded her. Lost in their depths, she would have willingly done anything he wanted to keep him looking at her that way forever.

"Can you stand on your own for a minute?"

Kelly nodded, bemused, and locked her knees.

"Good. I'm going to harness you into the swing. I don't want you hurting your wrists."

Blade moved away, and she heard him moving around behind her. Seconds later, she felt him securing a leather strap around her waist. She groaned at the feel of the leather touching her skin and his warm breath on her back.

When he began to attach a smaller version to each of her thighs, she looked down. She could see heavy metal rings on each side. More of the leather touched her bottom but she couldn't see it.

Kelly watched, mesmerized, as Blade moved around her once again. He attached two thick chains to the leather band around her waist, adjusting the chain to his satisfaction. The other ends of the chains hooked securely to the beams on the ceiling.

Without speaking a word, he unlocked her ankles from the floor and hooked chains to the rings on her thighs. Now that her thighs were no longer parted, she closed them tightly, trying to relieve the throbbing in her clit.

"No love. None of that." Blade chuckled as he produced a thick rod.

She couldn't take her eyes from it. *What was he going to do with that?*

"Easy love. It's just a spreader bar. I'm not going to beat you with it. Although…" He grinned at her teasingly.

"A spreader bar?"

Blade glanced up from where he attached the bar to the cuffs on her ankles.

"Yes. It will keep those gorgeous legs spread wide for me."

His slashing grin caused her heart to pound even faster. Oh Jeez. He made her crazy with need.

"Comfortable?"

At his question, her eyes flew open. She hadn't even realized she'd closed them. Shifting slightly, she realized that amazingly, she *was* comfortable. The padded leather didn't bother her at all and the chains no longer pulled at her arms. With a band around her back, she felt as comfortable as she would have sitting in a chair.

Well as comfortable as she would have been sitting in a chair completely naked with her legs spread and the most gorgeous man in the world standing between her spread thighs and intent on inspecting her body.

She saw he still waited for an answer and cleared her throat.

"Yes, I'm comfortable."

"Good. Now where was I?"

Her eyes fluttered closed of their own violation when Blade's thick finger touched a nipple. Jolting at the sensation, Kelly groaned. When both of his hands worked her nipples, her moans grew huskier and more continuous, but she couldn't stop.

"Look at me, Kelly."

Blade's harsh command penetrated the fog surrounding her and with considerable effort, she obeyed.

"Keep your eyes open and on mine."

Once again drawn into Blade's sharp gaze, her body tightened more with each caress. He stroked, tugged, and pinched her nipples relentlessly.

She had never felt like this before and soon became terrified of the feelings Blade created in her. Just as Kelly felt as though something inside her would snap, Blade removed his hands.

"No. No. Please. I need you to touch me. Please."

Sobbing unashamedly, she didn't care about anything except having Blade's hands back on her body. Shifting restlessly, she inadvertently caused her body to swing in the restraints.

Blade watched Kelly in wonder. He'd never in his life had a woman respond to him with such abandon this early in their play. Like a firecracker, Kelly flared up so completely and suddenly he'd had to stop playing with her breasts before he wanted to or she would have already exploded.

He'd known his self control would be put to the test with her. After all, he loved her, but he hadn't been prepared for such a dramatic response. Watching her eyes glaze over and the erotic sounds she made as her body shivered and trembled at his every touch had his cock hard enough to pound nails.

He, a Dom, for Christ's sake, already fought desperately not to come in his trousers at this fiery bit of femininity.

Her unexpected and uninhibited response thrilled him. She reacted as passionately with him as if they'd been doing this for years.

He wondered briefly if she would be like this with anyone who took his time with her.

"Easy, love. You're extremely undisciplined, aren't you? I can see a lot of punishments in your future."

Kelly felt Blade run his hands up and down her back and over her stomach with soothing strokes.

"Take deep breaths for me."

It took several seconds for Kelly to make sense of Blade's words. When she did, she obeyed, calming slightly. Her body still trembled, but some of the tightness had lessened.

She still ached and shuddered as Blade's hands learned her back and stomach. He spent long minutes stroking and soothing every square inch.

Kelly looked at Blade's face as he watched his hands move on her body. His hands moved over her stomach and chest, carefully avoiding her breasts.

His hands looked so dark and big as they slid over her damp body. Her pale skin looked flushed from his possessive touch.

That's how he touched her. With complete possession. He didn't ask. He didn't cajole. He touched every part of her as though memorizing her, stroking her with ownership and satisfaction, much like she'd seen Clay and Rio do with their prized horses.

He stroked, rubbed, fondled, and pinched whatever he wanted and short of using her safe word and being discarded from his life forever, Kelly couldn't do anything but submit to whatever he wanted to do to her.

Feeling even more moisture escape her saturated pussy, Kelly groaned. When Blade moved his attention to her feet, she looked down in amazement. Did he really intend to touch every single part of her?

Oh God. How would she ever be able to stand it when he finally got to her pussy?

Kelly felt a shiver go up her leg when Blade stroked her arch. Her foot looked so tiny in his large hands. It reminded her once again how really small and helpless she felt with him. Restrained like this, she felt even more so.

Why did the idea of being defenseless against Blade's strength excite her so much when it should have terrified her?

His hands moved up her calves, stroking and squeezing them, then continued up, running his fingers over the backs of her knees. Kelly groaned. She never knew she'd be so sensitive there.

When his hands continued their upward journey to her thighs, Kelly tried to close them against the powerful sensation his touch aroused. The spreader bar, however, kept her legs spread wide for Blade's continued perusal.

"You will be waxed here." Blade's fingertips grazed the soft curls covering her mound.

Kelly could feel the heat from his hand as he played with her curls. She arched into his hand as far as she could, whimpering with need. Her pussy continued to weep and her clit throbbed, so sensitive she couldn't stand it. Having no experience with desire like this, she floundered. Just when she thought she couldn't get any more aroused, Blade proved her wrong.

Her eyes popped open when Blade removed his hand and stood. Kelly automatically leaned toward him, craving the feel of his body touching hers.

"Did you hear me, Kelly?"

"W-what?" Kelly blinked, trying to focus.

Blade's lips twitched and she desperately wanted him to kiss her again.

"I want your pussy waxed. I want to be able to see you and feel you better."

He grinned at her again and her heart galloped.

"It will also make you more sensitive here." His fingers grazed her folds and she gasped.

"Oh, God. I'll never be able to stand it."

Blade chuckled as he leaned toward her. Feeling his warm breath on her hair, she lifted her face, parting her lips involuntarily inviting his kiss.

Chuckling again, he accommodated her.

His lips felt warm and firm on hers, sending spirals of pleasure through her body. His tongue swept her mouth, tangled with hers and explored as thoroughly as he'd explored the rest of her. When he ended the kiss, Kelly swayed and knew she would have fallen if she hadn't been secured by the leather straps.

Blade gazed at her tenderly as he framed her face with his strong hands. "You're absolutely stunning."

He gently pushed the hair back from her face. "Now that you've settled a little, I can continue. I'm going to raise you a bit, so I have better access."

At her startled look, he stroked her cheek softly. "Don't worry, love. I'll give you the orgasm your body is begging for, but not until I've explored you thoroughly."

Kelly felt her dripping pussy spasm and clench. How much longer could she bear it?

His eyes glittered darkly as they held hers.

"I'll give you what you need. *After* I get the knowledge I need."

"Anything," she panted. "Please, whatever you want. I can't stand it."

Blade raised her to the height he wanted, with her breasts level with his mouth. He pinched a nipple.

"You'll have to. Who does this body belong to?" he asked in a steely tone.

"You. It's all yours. All of me."

"Good girl." He finally released her nipple.

The sharp tingle had her eyes fluttering closed on a moan. Her whole body felt electrified, humming with an arousal that became razor sharp.

When Blade parted her folds, her breath caught. She looked down to see him studying her intently.

Running a finger over her, he murmured, "You're nice and wet for me, love. I want you to always be wet for me."

A thumb flicked over her clit caused her to buck, but Blade had obviously been expecting it because his grip held her firmly.

"I can't stand it!"

"You will," he murmured almost absently as he continued to explore her. "Your clit is red and throbbing nicely. Let's see if we can keep it that way."

Kelly groaned. She would never survive this. When she felt a thick blunt finger begin to push into her, she whimpered. She clenched on his finger as it entered her.

"You're extremely tight here, love. I can't wait to feel how tight you'll be when I finally work my cock into this pussy."

Kelly's harsh moans and whimpers never ceased as Blade's finger continued to move in and out of her.

"I want to, I want to, to feel, oh God!" He'd added another finger, stretching her.

"You want to feel what, love?"

When his fingers curled and stroked an extremely sensitive spot she hadn't even known existed, she cried out. He knew her body better than she did!

Kelly couldn't prevent her helpless cries as her body tightened more and more with each deliberate stroke. The pleasure kept building and building toward something she knew would shatter her.

Suddenly she clenched at emptiness as Blade abruptly withdrew from her.

"No. No. No, pleeease!" Kelly's eyes flew to Blade's desperately.

"You're too close, love," he crooned. "What did you want me to feel?"

Kelly looked at Blade's features and cursed his control. Except for the heat in his eyes and the impressive tenting of his trousers, he looked completely unaffected by what he did to her while she had become almost completely lost in it all.

"I want you to feel as crazy as you make me feel."

Blade's jaw clenched. "My control hasn't been tested so badly in years, Kelly. You respond beautifully to my every touch."

Kelly knew that only because she loved him could she trust him enough to respond the way she did. She couldn't let him know that yet. Once he knew of her feelings, it would be over. She tried to play it off, hoping he wouldn't suspect.

"You said that it was because I'm ready."

Blade's features tightened and for a split second, Kelly thought she saw a glimpse of anger in his eyes before he hid it. With a flash of intuition, she realized that only because his control had slipped had it showed.

Thrilled that she could shake him, but apprehensive at the anger she sensed in him, she watched him warily.

"You don't have to. I understand."

"Don't have to what, Kelly?"

"You know." Kelly could feel her face flame.

"No, I don't," Blade snapped. "Say it, then be quiet, so I can finish."

"You don't have to make me come," she blurted.

Blade's smile only scared her more.

"Oh, you'll come, Kelly. You'll learn quickly that I keep all my promises. Something you'll want to remember for the future."

Kelly frowned. "But you stopped."

"I did. I don't want you to come until I've finished, and I'm tired of explaining myself to you. You are getting away with quite a bit because this is your first time. Don't think that I will allow such things in the future."

Kelly's face burned. "But I don't understand. You've touched me everywhere, touched everything."

"No, love. I haven't even begun exploring that gorgeous ass of yours."

Kelly couldn't prevent her gasp. "No. Please, no." Shaking with terror, her eyes begged him.

Blade moved closer, wrapping his arms around her and began stroking her back.

"Sshhh, love. Everything will be all right. You trust me, don't you?"

"But it hurts so much!"

"What does it feel like?"

"Like I'm being ripped in half. Please, Blade, not this. Anything else, just not this," she wailed.

Blade pulled back slightly and studied her. She felt his hands, strong and warm on her back, but his face blurred as her eyes filled with tears.

"I know what I'm doing, my love. The pain you'll feel from me will only bring you more pleasure. Erotic pain, love. Not cruel."

Blade continued to study her. Kelly wasn't sure what he saw, but he seemed to come to some sort of decision.

"I'm going to get you past this, love. To do this, I'm going to do something I've never done before."

Blade took a deep breath as he continued to watch her and for the first time she thought she saw a slight uneasiness in him.

"I'm taking away your safe word for this."

He ignored her cries and continued.

"No matter what, I won't stop until I've finished. You can cry, scream, or shout your safe word at the top of your lungs and I won't stop."

"No! Please!" Kelly wailed.

Blade once again stroked her back soothingly.

"You came to me because you trust me, Kelly. Remember that."

With that, his hands began a slow journey down her back until they reached her buttocks. She stiffened and braced herself for the pain.

Feeling his teeth nip at her breast startled her. When his tongue soothed over the slight sting and his mouth closed over a nipple, Kelly felt the tug all the way to her womb.

His mouth continued to wreak havoc on her senses. He used his tongue and teeth to rebuild her arousal that fear had all but destroyed.

While his mouth stayed busy on her uplifted breasts, Blade's hands kept moving, stroking and kneading every inch of her buttocks.

Before long before her body once again teetered on the edge. When his mouth left her breasts, the loss of his touch had her crying out in denial.

One of Blade's hands left her rear and seconds later she felt his fingers push once again into her pussy. With her legs spread wide apart, she couldn't squeeze them together on his hand the way she wanted to. His thumb circled her sensitive clit, not quite touching her where she needed it most.

"Please, Blade. I need…"

"I know exactly what you need. You're going to come with my fingers in your ass."

"*No!*" Kelly twisted frantically, but with Blade holding her bottom in his strong hands and his fingers inside her pussy, she couldn't move an inch.

"Yes!" Fingers once again pressed on that ultra sensitive spot inside her until she whimpered helplessly. He used his knowledge of her body to drive everything but the pleasure he gave her out of her mind.

"I'm going to use this sweet juice dripping from your pussy to lube your ass."

"Nooo!"

When Blade's fingers left her pussy, she stiffened fearfully, only to beg when they skimmed over her clit.

"Ohhh! More! Please more!"

She felt him next to her, his breath hot on her raised arms. He had one hand over her mound, using his fingers to tease her clit enough to drive her insane, pushing her closer and closer, but not allowing her the relief her body craved.

Oh, her clit throbbed.

Her pussy clenched frantically and she squeezed her eyes tightly against it.

When she felt his finger trace the crease of her bottom, her breath caught.

He was touching her there!

She felt him spread moisture around her tight hole. Nerve endings came alive as he began to push into her forbidden passage and she cried out.

"You're very tight here, love. Too tight."

Kelly tightened as he stroked in and out of her, pushing into her a little more with each stroke. Moaning continuously, she felt her body open to him.

"That's it, love. Now I'm going to add another finger."

"Oh God!"

"It will pinch just a bit and burn. Erotic pain only, love. You're being such a good girl. You're going to be rewarded for being so good."

Kelly felt Blade withdraw his fingers, felt the way her body tried to hold him in. Before she could process it, he pushed back into her with two thick fingers.

"*It hurts.*"

"Relax, love. Let it have you. Let *me* have you."

Kelly had no choice, spread and bent this way. She had no defense against him as he stroked in and out of her tight hole, gaining ground with each thrust.

"Your ass is so tight," Blade gritted. "How does it feel, Kelly? How does it feel to have my fingers invading your most private opening and there isn't a thing you can do to stop me?"

"It's too much, too forbidden," Kelly told him in a voice she didn't recognize as her own. "I feel full and helpless and wild."

She gasped when Blade thrust his two fingers fully inside her. With his other hand, he continued to circle her painfully throbbing clit, almost but not quite touching it, and her mind ceased to function.

She could only *feel.* He'd completely taken her over. Whatever Blade wanted to do to her, whatever he wanted, he could have.

She couldn't stop clenching on his fingers, amazed that the burning sensation she felt only drove her higher. Nerve endings jumped with pleasure and need and hunger. Soon she wanted more.

"More! Harder! Faster!"

"Does it burn, love?"

"Oh, yes!"

"Think about how much it's going to burn when I work my cock into your tight ass," Blade hissed.

"Yes! Oh God, anything!" She couldn't believe she'd never felt like this before and wanted this feeling to last forever.

When his hand shifted, suddenly it became too much.

"*No!*"

"Yes! Come for me."

As Blade massaged her clit steadily, Kelly lurched. Held immobile she had no choice but to give in.

Her scream filled the room as she had the first orgasm of her life. Blade's strokes on her clit never faltered and when she felt the intense burn she clamped down on his fingers, and another orgasm quickly followed.

Trembling so badly, she heard the chains rattle, she cried out, "*No more. Please. I can't!*"

"One more, Kelly."

"No."

"Yes!"

Blade's fingers on her too sensitive clit continued their torment while the fingers wedged in her bottom began to stroke in and out of her, gathering moisture from her dripping slit to make the glide easier.

"I'm going to spend a lot of time stretching this ass for my cock."

Blade's harsh words made her shiver. Feeling how tight she felt with him using just two fingers inside her, she could only imagine what it would feel like when he pushed his cock into her.

Without warning, another orgasm hit her, robbing her of breath. Blade controlled her movements, ruthlessly drawing it out until she collapsed weakly in the restraints. Finally, the stroking on her clit ceased and she began to breathe.

She couldn't prevent the involuntary shudder as Blade withdrew from her.

"Easy, love. I've got you."

Kelly felt Blade's arm like a steel band wrap around her waist as he unfastened her restraints. When he released her arms, she automatically wrapped them around his neck as she slumped forward. When he finished, he held her in his strong arms and moved to one of the padded benches.

She felt his rock hard erection press against her bottom. Self conscious of sitting in his lap completely naked while he remained fully dressed, she frowned.

"What about you?" Her whisper sounded hoarse, her throat raw from her screams.

"What about me?" Blade's voice sounded tight with tension. Thrilled that he desired her, she wanted to give him at least some of the pleasure he had given her.

"You're hard," she blurted.

"Don't worry, Kelly. It will be taken care of."

By whom?

She almost blurted out the thought but feared his answer.

"But I thought..."

"You thought what? That I would ease it by fucking you?"

Kelly winced. He obviously wanted her. The proof prodded against her bottom. His tone, though, sounded harsh, the anger he'd shown earlier had returned.

Not sure what she'd done to make him angry, she nevertheless wanted to make amends.

Still red, Kelly nodded. "Yes, I thought you wanted me. Just like I want you." She stroked his face tenderly.

Blade laughed coldly. "You said it yourself. You're ready. Anyone with patience and knowledge of a woman's body could have done what I just did."

"No. Blade I…"

Blade stood and released her, steadying her on her feet before moving away.

"Get dressed, Kelly. I'll wait for you in the sitting room."

Without looking at her, he turned and walked out the door.

What should she do? Blade seemed angry at the thought that she would respond to anyone else. Had he gotten jealous? Did that mean he actually cared?

Quickly dismissing that idea, Kelly gathered her clothes and moved to the adjoining bathroom to clean up before dressing.

Should she tell him how she felt? Or, had he become angry because she had disobeyed him so many times. Knowing he dealt with more sophisticated women who knew how to act in a situation like this, Kelly felt gauche and insecure, fat and clumsy.

Besides, if she told Blade the way she felt now, he would never believe her. He would probably think she'd reacted to the way he'd made her feel.

No. She couldn't tell him now. She'd wait until the right opportunity came up and she could be sure that he would believe her and that her love would be welcome.

Her decision made, she strode to the door, hoping she remembered the way back. It would be easy to get lost in a place this size.

Why hadn't Blade waited for her?

Stepping out into the hallway, she found the very formal butler who'd let her in.

"Hello. Sebastian, isn't it?"

"Yes, Mademoiselle Kelly. If you'll come with me, please. Master Blade is waiting."

Hearing the man who'd just forced three orgasms from her body referred to as 'Master' made Kelly's pulse skyrocket.

Nodding shyly, Kelly followed Sebastian to the elevator, uncomfortably aware that he had to know what she and Blade had been doing up here. Only a few minutes passed before the French butler escorted her back into the sitting room.

"I talked to him until I was blue in the face when he visited, but this asshole doesn't listen."

Kelly recognized Royce's deep voice before she saw him. She'd never heard that tone from him before. Usually his voice sounded like dark silk, not this frustrated anger.

Royce sat in the sitting room, along with King, both talking to Blade.

The three owners of Club Desire might be different in looks, but they all had an aura of power that surrounded them.

The way they held their bodies, the sharpness of their eyes and their commanding presence, all but shouted it. When three sets of those all knowing eyes turned in her direction, she felt like a deer caught in headlights.

Jeez, if she could bottle that, she and Jesse would be set for life.

"Kelly, you know Royce and King, don't you?" Blade moved to stand beside her, his hand hot on her waist even through her dress, reminding her what it had felt like on her bare skin.

"We've meet before. They're not exactly customers. Yet. Nice to see you both again."

"Yes, I heard that you're working on men's products. Good luck with it."

Royce's smooth tone, Kelly knew, drove women wild. With his long black curls, deep green eyes, and lean muscular build, he looked more beautiful than any movie star. Usually all smiles and charm, she'd heard he had a fiery temper when provoked.

Although beautiful, he left Kelly cold. She wanted only Blade.

"How have you been, Kelly?"

King Taylor's low gravelly voice fit him perfectly. He stood only about an inch shorter than both Blade and Royce, but where the other men had leanly muscled bodies, King looked huge.

She'd heard he'd started lifting weights as a teenager because he'd been told he'd be too scrawny to work with the horses on his father's ranch. He'd worked hard to become the kind of man his father would have been proud of, and she knew he must have been devastated that his father thought him weak.

He'd obviously worked hard to change that because now he looked thickly muscled all over.

His dark blonde hair had been cut shorter than the other men's, just barely reaching his collar. Too rugged looking to be called handsome, he looked fierce, but everyone knew how gentle he could be. A woman would feel protected and cherished in those thickly corded arms.

The only arms that Kelly wanted around her, though, were Blade's.

"I'm fine, King. And you?"

"Fine, Kelly," he replied absently, obviously frustrated. He sighed. "Sorry, honey. I'm good, thanks." He smiled at her kindly. "Would you like something to drink?"

"Water would be great," she smiled her thanks. Her throat felt parched and sore from her screams of pleasure.

"I'll get it." Blade moved to a small built in refrigerator she hadn't noticed. Cracking open a bottle, he poured water into a heavy crystal glass and handed it to her as he led her to a leather sofa.

"We'll only be a few more minutes, Kelly."

Kelly flushed. Apparently interrupting a meeting, she started to rise, but Blade stopped her with a firm grip on her wrist.

"Sit down, Kelly. We have a few things to discuss."

Kelly sank back to the sofa, automatically responding to the command in his voice, glancing at him nervously before lifting the glass to her lips.

What did he want to discuss? Was he angry enough to end their agreement? If so, what would she do?

"…several times since he left," Kelly heard Blade say to the others, effectively jerking her thoughts back to the present.

"I'd love to cut him off, but it sounds like he has a woman all lined up to be his sub." Blade sighed tiredly as he ran his hand over the back of his neck. "The women he's *practiced* on so far have all deserted him after only a session or two."

"He's hurting them," King said through clenched teeth.

"Yes, I'm sure he is," Blade replied tightly. "I'm doing my best to spread the word in the Virginia area through our connections there to warn the subs about him. But whoever this woman is that he's apparently obsessed with, she's not a sub."

"What?" Royce looked ready to spit nails. "Do you mean this idiot has designs on a woman, one he wants to master, and she knows nothing about it and isn't even a sub?"

"That about covers it." Blade stood and strode to the bar, pouring three neat whiskeys. Handing one to each of the other men, he tossed his own back with a grimace. "He hits the chat room almost every day around two o'clock. Maybe one of you can get through to him."

Their concern floored her. She didn't realize the kinds of things these men dealt with on a daily basis. She had assumed their lives were nothing more than a series of sexual fun and games. The distress they felt, worry for some unknown woman showed clearly.

They talked for several more minutes about ways to get through to this 'Dom', finished their drinks, and with murmured goodbyes, Royce and King walked out, leaving her alone with Blade.

Aware of his eyes on her, she looked up and saw the fresh knowledge in his gaze as it moved over her. Weak after all he'd done to her, she felt more vulnerable than ever. Even sated, her body responded to his nearness, the heated look in his eyes. Her nipples pebbled under his gaze, still very sensitive, and when his lips twitched, Kelly realized he knew the effect he had on her.

When he walked toward her, she noticed his arousal tenting his dark trousers alarmingly.

"Are you sure-," Kelly began, staring at the tenting.

"You will not be taking care of it, Kelly. You're not ready for my cock yet."

"But--"

"I'm in charge here, Kelly, not you. Or are you trying to back out already?"

She breathed a sigh of relief that Blade didn't want out of their agreement. With her body still humming from the pleasure he'd just recently given her, she knew she didn't want to go without it or him ever again.

"No."

Blade nodded and reached into his pocket. He pulled out a beautiful gold choker, inlaid with black onyx and what appeared to be diamonds. Of course, they couldn't be real. He probably used it for the women he trained.

She'd heard from Nat Langley, her partner Jesse's sister, that all Doms in Desire had a different design. They each wore a ring on their right hand and duplicated that design on the choker they gave the woman they eventually claimed.

Her eyes automatically went to the diamond and onyx ring Blade wore.

"By wearing this for the next six weeks, you're agreeing to belong to me and to obey me. If you choose to disobey me, it is with the knowledge that you will be punished in any way I see fit. Using your safe word will be the only way to stop me. Once that's used, however, we are through. Our arrangement is over."

Blade sat next to her, watching her steadily.

"I mean it, Kelly. Either you trust me to know what you can handle and gradually lead you to what you're not yet ready for, or you don't. Also, you now have two safe words. Red light and yellow light. Red light, as I've already mentioned, means stop. No matter what I'm doing, I will stop immediately. Since the next six weeks will be spent slowly increasing your experiences, it would only be used if you are scared."

Blade grasped her chin and lifted her face to his. "There will be nothing to fear, and you'll only let fear get the best of you if you don't trust me. Trust is everything in a relationship like ours. There will be no lies between us."

Kelly felt herself flush. She forced herself to remain still when she would have shifted uncomfortably. If Blade noticed, he didn't comment.

"What's yellow light?"

Blade smiled darkly. "It means that you need me to slow down. If you find you're having trouble adjusting to whatever I'm doing, just say 'yellow light' and I'll slow down. Any more questions?"

"I don't think so," she replied breathlessly.

"Good." Blade pulled her across his lap and took her mouth in a kiss so tender and possessive, Kelly melted.

Her hands crept around his neck and grasped handfuls of his silky black hair. It felt so good to be in his arms like this.

It felt so incredible to be kissed so thoroughly, so tenderly, by the man she loved with all her heart. Held close to his chest, Kelly's eyes began to well with tears. She'd never felt so safe and secure.

When Blade lifted his head, Kelly forced her eyes open.

"I'll be sending over something for you to wear tomorrow night. We're going over to the hotel for dinner."

He lifted her chin. "Wear exactly what I send. No more. No less. Understood?"

"Yes, Blade," she responded docilely.

With a last lingering kiss, he helped her to her feet.

"Do you accept my collar, love? Will you wear this everywhere you go for the next six weeks?"

"Yes, Blade. I will." She wished she would be wearing it for a lifetime, but smiled, happy for the chance to wear it now. She kept her eyes lowered, so Blade wouldn't see the love she knew shone in them when he clasped the choker around her neck. It felt surprisingly comfortable, but heavy enough that she would be constantly aware of its presence.

"Come on, love. Let's get something to eat at the diner and I'll take you home."

Later that night, curled in her bed, Kelly thought about Blade and what he'd taught her about herself.

He'd dropped her off with another of those devastating kisses and an order to get a good night's sleep. Then he left, promising to pick her up tomorrow night at seven.

Tracing her fingers over the choker she still wore, she smiled.

She'd finally started to get on with her life. Somehow she'd found the nerve to approach Blade and found herself brave enough to agree to turning over control to him for the next six weeks.

Smiling in the darkness, Kelly closed her eyes. She couldn't wait for tomorrow night and all the nights she would be in Blade's arms.

Chapter Four

The next day was Jesse's Saturday off. Kelly and Jesse took turns having Saturdays off since hiring the two high school girls several weeks ago. Katy and Brittany worked hard and the customers loved them. They also drew a lot of the younger crowd.

Teenage girls loved the more subtle fragrances and their boyfriends got a big kick out of the array of scents.

Kelly helped yet another customer, glad that Saturdays kept her busy. She desperately needed the distraction to keep her mind off of tonight. Even busy, though, thoughts of Blade kept intruding, especially after a delivery came for her shortly after she'd opened the store that morning.

She'd immediately taken it up to her apartment and placed it on her bed. She'd resisted the urge to open it. Picturing herself in whatever Blade had sent would have made her crazy all day.

Seeing that the girls easily handled the customers, she caught their attention and gestured that she would be in the back room.

Loyal customers from where she and Jesse used to have their store in Maryland still ordered by phone and Kelly had orders to box for shipping.

When she walked into the back room, she saw Frank carefully emptying the cabinets in what used to be a kitchen and putting everything on folding tables set up along the far wall.

"Oh, Frank. I forgot."

Just then, a laughing Jesse walked through the back door. Rio smiled and swatted her bottom as he came in behind her, carrying yet another folding table. Clay followed, chuckling at the two and shaking his head at their antics. Two men that Kelly had only met recently brought up the rear.

Boone and Chase Jackson, she'd learned, had grown up in Desire with Clay and Rio, but had left the town right after Chase, the youngest, graduated from high school. First class builders, they'd made their fortunes building luxury condos, high dollar homes, and shopping malls.

Jesse learned from her husbands that something had happened that made the two men sell everything and come back to Desire. They had helped Clay and Rio build the house they now lived in with Jesse.

Boone and Chase didn't have to work, having made enough to live quite comfortably for the rest of their lives in Desire but loved to keep busy working with their hands. They'd soon become Desire's handymen and got called to do everything from building houses to unclogging toilets.

Turning her attention from the men, Kelly watched Jesse with her husbands and smiled. Her friend absolutely glowed with happiness. Love for Clay and Rio shone from her eyes and it they obviously both adored her.

Kelly would give anything to see Blade look at her that way.

"Kelly?" Jesse's voice pulled her from her thoughts.

"Ummm?"

"Is everything okay?" Kelly avoided Jesse's searching gaze and saw that both Clay and Rio's eyes had sharpened.

"Everything's fine," Kelly smiled at her friend reassuringly. "I just forgot that the new cabinets were coming in today until just a few minutes ago."

Kelly forced herself not to squirm under their combined scrutiny.

"We talked about this yesterday, Kelly."

"Yes, I know. I just forgot. It's not a big deal."

She grimaced when Jesse frowned at her. "What's wrong, Kelly?"

Kelly saw Jesse's eyes widen when she noticed the choker around her neck. "Did you get everything done last night that you wanted to do?"

Clay and Rio stood with their hands on their hips, unashamedly listening to every word. Silently thanking Jesse for not revealing their conversation about Blade, Kelly nodded.

"Yes, I did."

Kelly sighed in relief when Jesse nodded and mouthed, *we'll talk later,* and turned to her husbands.

"Are you two going to get to work on my cabinets or are you just here to sniff my products," she teased.

Kelly watched both men flick a glance at their wife before turning their attention back to her.

Kelly shifted nervously when they continued to stare at her.

"Is there something you want to tell us, honey?" Clay asked softly.

Kelly knew that tone. She'd been around Jesse several times when Clay had used that tone with her and knew not to trust it.

"No." Kelly shook her head, hoping he would drop it. She should have known better.

Both Clay and Rio considered themselves her protectors and took the position very seriously. The men in Desire had long ago insisted that all women who lived here had to be under a man's protection. Although *all* the men who lived here protected the women, most women had a man or men who took responsibility for them and guarded them very closely.

Usually reserved for a woman's husband or husbands, the responsibility of being her protector had been taken by Clay and Rio because she'd moved to Desire for Jesse.

They took the responsibility far too seriously and Kelly didn't want a lot of questions about her relationship with Blade. If they found out about her agreement with him, they would be livid.

She didn't know what the two of them would do if they found out she'd gone to the club. She'd have to talk to Blade about it tonight. She hated lying to them, but she needed this chance with Blade.

For several long seconds, Clay and Rio both studied her. Even Boone and Chase, leaning back against the counter with their arms folded over their wide chests, watched attentively.

"You're wearing Blade's collar." Clay said through clenched teeth. "Apparently we'll have to go see him."

With a scorching glance at Kelly and a look that promised retribution directed at Jesse, Clay stormed out.

"Oh, no!" Kelly groaned. She looked at Jesse fearfully. "What am I going to do? Can't you stop him?"

"Stop Clay?" Jesse asked incredulously to the amusement of both Boone and Chase. They still chuckled as Rio approached Kelly.

"We're only trying to look out for you, honey." When he grasped her arms, Kelly's eyes flew to his. "I want you to promise that you'll come to me if you need help."

"I will," Kelly nodded hesitantly.

"I mean it, Kelly. We'll both be watching you like hawks."

At the sound of Clay's truck tearing out of the parking lot, Rio grimaced. "Give me your keys, Kelly. I'd better go stop Clay from killing Blade before we get the answers we need."

Kelly turned and lifted her keys from the hook on the wall.

"You won't let him hurt Blade, will you?" she couldn't help asking as he started for the door.

Rio glanced back at her over his shoulder. "That depends on his answers."

Almost two hours passed before Clay and Rio came back. Clay walked in and Kelly, who'd been listening for them from the front, hurried to the back to see what had happened.

Jesse had just finished addressing the last of the boxes she and Kelly had packed for shipping. Chase, who'd been flirting with both women shamelessly the whole time, winked at Kelly.

"Come on, Jesse. Ditch Rio and Clay and come live with us. Boone and I are younger and have a lot more stamina than those two ugly husbands of yours. Oh, Clay, Rio, back so soon?"

Rio walked in just as Clay growled, "Stay away from my woman." He lifted Jesse off her feet and kissed her hungrily.

"You trying to steal our woman?" Rio asked with a mock frown while moving to Jesse for his kiss.

"Been at it with both of them since you left," Boone muttered. "Can't get a lick of work out of him."

Of course, no one believed him. The old cabinets and countertop had already been removed and they had started on installing the new ones.

"What happened?" Kelly asked Clay anxiously when he released Jesse to Rio.

His face tightened. "We talked to Blade."

Kelly glanced at Jesse, who started toward her. Rio pulled his wife against his chest.

Kelly turned back to Clay. "And?"

Clay folded his arms over his chest and stared at her. "When Jesse first came to Desire, Jake, as Jesse's brother in law immediately became her protector. Jesse and Nat had gone shopping and got a flat tire." He turned to frown at his wife. "Nat had already called Jake and knew we'd be there. But, Jesse decided to change it herself and had already started when Jake, Rio and I pulled up. Jake made her stop. She could have been hurt and Jake had every right to turn her over his knee and paddle her ass. Rio and I couldn't have done a thing to stop it."

His lips twitched. "Right now, Blade feels what we felt that day."

Of their own violation, Kelly's hands moved to cover her bottom. She looked at Clay in horror.

"You wouldn't!"

When Clay merely raised a brow, Kelly turned pleading eyes to Jesse.

"Jesse, damn it! Do something!"

Hiding a smile, Jesse winked at her and whispered something to Rio. He smiled dangerously and released her to go to Clay. Kelly noticed Rio's eyes never left Jesse's jean clad bottom as she reached up and pulled Clay's head down to whisper in his ear.

Both of Clay's brows shot up at whatever Jesse had said to him and with a grin, he straightened.

Without a word, Rio moved to Jesse, flung her, laughing and wiggling, over his shoulder and went out the door. Kelly couldn't help but notice that both men now sported impressive erections and their features had tightened with desire, the same way Blade's had been last night when he'd released her from the restraints.

Just as she thought of him, he burst through the back door looking desperate. She saw his relief when he spotted her and frowned at Clay as he moved to stand between her and his friend defensively.

Boone and Chase, of course, had stopped working and looked on in amusement at the scene unfolding before them.

"Damn it, Clay."

"You have Jesse to thank for distracting me from giving Kelly the spanking she deserves," Clay told Blade ruthlessly. "You know I have every right to do it."

"Not if I claim her." Blade's softly spoken words echoed in the dead silence of the room.

"Are you claiming her?"

"Yes." Blade's replied swiftly.

Kelly peered around Blade in time to see Clay's lips twitch.

Both Boone and Chase looked incredulous.

Kelly felt bubbles of delight burst inside her.

Blade had claimed her!

Clay smiled in satisfaction, but warned, "If you hurt her, I'll have to hurt you."

Blade nodded at the larger man unflinchingly. "Understood."

Hearing his truck engine roar to life, Clay winked at Kelly and headed for the door. "Gotta go."

Kelly looked up when Blade turned to face her. "Hi."

"Hi, yourself."

She closed her eyes when she felt Blade's lips on her forehead and heard Boone tell Chase, "I guess she's off limits, too."

Kelly's eyes fluttered open when Blade lifted his head and turned sharply to Chase.

"Have you been messing with my woman?"

Chase grinned at Blade. "Define messing."

Apparently knowing Chase well, Blade chuckled and turned to Boone.

"Can't you do anything with your brother?"

"Are you kidding? He flirts with every woman in town. One of these days, some husband is gonna come after him and teach him a lesson."

"Then all the women will feel sorry for me and spoil me rotten," Chase retorted with a leer.

Blade circled an arm around Kelly and pulled her close.

"I think a better revenge will be when you two find a woman and settle down. I wonder what Chase will do when every man in town flirts with *his* woman."

Shocked, Kelly shot a look at Blade when both Boone and Chase's smiles fell and their eyes took on a haunted look.

"I don't think that's ever gonna happen," Boone said softly. "Come on Chase, let's get some work done."

When Kelly started to speak, Blade shook his head warningly.

"Come with me," Blade told her with a glance at his friends. "Then, I have to leave. I'm going to be late for my appointment with Rachel. She's doing something for me."

Kelly's eyes widened in amazement when both Boone and Chase spun, their stances threatening as they faced Blade.

"What is Rachel doing for you?" Boone asked tightly.

Not looking at all threatened, Blade smiled darkly. "That's between Rachel and me. Why do you care anyway? Oh, by the way, she did mention to me that she needed more organized storage, like this." He gestured toward the cabinets. "Rachel told me she can't afford it right now, but she needs space for her panties."

Blade smirked, ignoring the dangerous glitter in Boone's eyes and the way Chase's fists clenched spasmodically at his sides. "Rachel sure does have a wonderful assortment of panties, lots of colors and styles. She really does need more storage for them, you know, a way to keep the thongs and the crotchless panties separate."

Pretty sure that Blade talked about the lingerie store that Rachel owned needing the storage, Kelly wondered why he worded it in such a way that it sounded personal.

Why did both Boone and Chase look like they wanted to kill him?

"Come on, Kelly. I want to talk to you."

Blade folded her hand in his and led her out the back door. Once outside he turned and pulled her roughly against him. "You belong to me. I claimed you. You didn't deny my claim. And you owe me. If I hadn't claimed you, you would have found yourself over Clay's lap. I wouldn't have liked that and neither would you. The only lap you're going to be over is mine!"

When he ground his mouth against hers, Kelly felt her breasts swell, and her nipples hardened to poke at his chest. Lust sizzled through her.

Like before, Blade used his mouth ruthlessly, demanding submission to him, forcing her to open and give him complete access. And, like before, Kelly found herself swept away, unable to deny his demands.

When Blade lifted his head, his eyes glittered darkly.

Kelly searched his face and knew she had to ask. "Is keeping Clay from spanking me the only reason you claimed me?" He studied her for several moments and she wished she could read his mind.

"No," he finally replied, "but what does it matter? You'd already agreed to belong to me for six weeks." He shrugged. "After that I can turn you back over to Clay and Rio."

Kelly frowned when he mentioned turning the responsibility of her protection back over to Clay and Rio and he waited to see if she would protest. When she said nothing, it made him wonder again if he'd been mistaken in her feelings for him.

He knew that he had no intention of renouncing his claim, but she couldn't know that.

She didn't need to know that he had already fallen for her and vowed to keep her. She certainly didn't need any declarations of love from him.

Right now she needed the knowledge that she could get over what her fucking ex boyfriend had done to her.

She didn't need any emotional demands from him. Still vulnerable, she could very well confuse desire for something more. She would respond to anyone with patience and knowledge. He didn't want her mistaking the desire he could make her feel with love for him.

First, he had to do away with her inhibitions, get past all the horrors of physical intimacy that haunted her.

Then, he'd find a way to know what her true feelings were.

But for now...

"Did you open the box I sent?"

"No." Kelly blushed.

"Why not?"

Kelly felt a shiver of apprehension go through her when Blade's face hardened and he lifted her chin.

"If you think you're going to get out of our agreement..."

"No," Kelly said hurriedly. "I just wanted to wait until after work." She glanced up at him from beneath lowered lashes to find him staring at her. "I was, um, afraid that I would spend all day imagining, well, you know."

Another glance found Blade grinning deviously.

"Imagining yourself dressed as I ordered and wondering what I'm going to do to you?"

She nodded as her face burned. "I'm already nervous. I didn't want to make it worse."

"Ahh. Well in that case I probably shouldn't tell you that there's a chain in the box that I want you to put aside for me to put on you when I get here."

"Blade, you shouldn't buy me jewelry." She lifted her fingers to trace the choker she wore.

"It gives me pleasure to see you marked with my brand," Blade told her arrogantly, running his own finger over the choker. He lowered his voice conspiratorially. "The chain will give you a great deal of pleasure, therefore pleasing me. Be ready on time."

With a last hard kiss, he turned and walked back to his truck, whistling.

Kelly absently brushed her fingers over her swollen lips. Running her tongue over them, she found she could still taste Blade there.

Already aroused, Kelly looked at her watch and grimaced. She still had another five hours to wait.

Freshly showered, Kelly carefully smoothed on her vanilla scented lotion, all the while glancing apprehensively at the white box sitting on her bed. Finishing with the lotion, she reached for the powder. After dipping the feather applicator into the shimmering powder, she applied it all over, wondering what Blade's reaction would be.

The powder she'd created was not only scented, but flavored, and it gave the wearer's skin a subtle shimmer. Feathering it over her breasts, she imagined Blade's surprise when he took a nipple in his mouth and tasted sweet vanilla. Everywhere she applied it, she imagined Blade's mouth there and she'd become more than a little aroused by the time she'd finished.

She'd left her hair down, hoping to please Blade and had already applied the light makeup she'd recently started wearing.

She couldn't put it off any longer.

Placing a hand over her stomach, she took a calming breath and moved to the box. Her heart raced as she reached for the lid.

Pushing aside the tissue paper, Kelly carefully lifted the item on top. She pulled out an absolutely beautiful, simply cut black dress. Strapless and made of silk, the material gathered over the bodice, crisscrossing over the top and crossing again around the waist in the back, then tied in a bow at the front.

The waist nipped down to a full skirt which looked as if it would fall right above her knees.

Kelly eyed the dress in confusion. She loved it but had thought Blade would have picked out something a little more revealing for their date.

Shrugging, she carefully laid the dress on the bed and reached into the box again. This is what she'd expected. The black corset felt smooth, without lace or frills. The cups looked awfully small, though.

Kelly donned the corset and stared at herself in the mirror. Her mouth fell open in shock.

Was that her?

Now she saw why the cups had looked so small. Their only purpose appeared to be shelves for her breasts.

The cups only lifted her breasts. They pushed her breasts high, leaving her nipples exposed. Her waist looked impossibly small as the corset hugged her figure, flaring out to her hips before ending just above the blonde curls covering her mound.

Turning, she saw that her bottom had been left completely exposed except for the garter straps down the middle of each of the globes of her ass.

A thorough search of the box produced no panties. Remembering Blade's words, she realized with a jolt of excitement that she wouldn't be permitted to wear panties tonight.

The stockings felt silky and the sheer black made her legs look amazing.

She slipped the dress over her head and retied it, crossing the material in the back and ending with the bow off center in front.

Slipping her feet into surprisingly comfortable high heeled pumps with little velvet bows on the sides, Kelly looked back into the white box.

Only a small black velvet box remained. Opening it, she saw the chain Blade had told her about. Frowning, she studied it. Gold and long, about twenty four inches, it had little rings on each end. Above each ring she saw a tiny gold screw.

What in the world?

The sharp knock on the door startled her so much she nearly dropped the chain. Knowing Blade wouldn't like to be kept waiting, she hurried for the door and flung it open. Her breath caught when she saw him.

She'd never seen Blade dressed in a suit before. His crisp white shirt against his dark skin looked devastating. His silky hair, dark as his suit, hung loose on his shoulders.

"You look beautiful, love," he murmured silkily. "Aren't you going to invite me in?"

"What? Oh! Yes, I'm sorry." Kelly felt the butterflies in her stomach become dive bombers. "You look very handsome," she told him, stunned by the huskiness in her voice.

"Oh, I see you have the chain ready for me. Good girl. Put your hands on my shoulders and keep them there."

Kelly reached up and held his wide shoulders, feeling the play of muscles as he reached for her. Untying the bow at her waist, he moved the material to the back where it crisscrossed, and undid it, pulling it back to the front where it hung from the cups of the bodice.

Grasping the material over her breasts, he tugged and Kelly felt the cups give way.

"Oh." Startled, she looked down, amazed that he would tear such a beautiful dress when she hadn't even worn it yet.

But the dress hadn't torn. A row of snaps she hadn't seen ran along both sides. Her breasts, now bared to him, flushed and her nipples pebbled over the top of the corset.

"Beautiful," Blade breathed as he produced the chain and draped it over the back of her neck, leaving the two ends hanging in front.

He looked at her breasts hungrily and for the first time in years, Kelly was thankful to be so well endowed. She'd always thought of herself as chubby, especially next to someone as tall and willowy as Jesse, but the way Blade looked at her made her feel beautiful and desirable.

When he bent his head to take a pebbled nipple into his mouth, Kelly pressed her thighs together against the sharp tug in her womb.

"Mmm, vanilla," Blade rumbled, nipping her with his sharp teeth. "I never liked vanilla anything until now."

When Blade shifted his attention to her other breast she writhed in his arms, trying to pull him closer. When he lifted his head, Kelly felt bereft and a whimper escaped her throat.

"Put your hands back on my shoulders, love."

Kelly opened her eyes and, surprised to find her fingers tangled in his hair. Shakily she let go of the silky darkness, allowing him to straighten. She stared at him, dazed, and his tender smile and knowing eyes told her he knew just what he did to her.

"Now, let's get your chain attached, so we can go to dinner. I'm starving."

How could he think of food now?

"You're torturing me," she groaned.

"Love, I haven't even begun to torture you. Let's start with this."

Kelly watched helplessly as Blade slipped one of the rings at the end of the chain over a pointed nipple. He used the tiny screw to tighten the ring and Kelly gasped as the slight bite arrowed straight to her weeping slit.

She bit her lip and moaned as Blade tightened the ring to his satisfaction before moving to her other breast. Her eyes closed on a moan as her nails dug into his shoulders. Breathing heavily, she fought to remain upright.

"Let's go, love."

Kelly's eyes snapped open. Blinking, she found the bodice back in place, and the length of material once again tied around her waist to a smart little bow in front.

A look in the mirror showed he'd put her back together without her even being aware of it. Her gaze slid over the chain which hung around her neck on either side of the choker she wore.

The chain didn't look like a necklace as it didn't form a complete loop. She turned to Blade.

"Everyone will know where this chain is attached," she told him worriedly.

"Of course they will, love, especially when they see me playing with it."

Kelly closed her eyes as a wave of longing washed over her. She never knew a man could be so inventive and intent on arousing a woman. "I won't be able to stand it. It feels like your fingers are pinching my nipples. I can't go out like this!"

"Are you using your safe word?" he challenged.

"No!"

"We'll see how long it takes before you do," Blade replied enigmatically and led her from the apartment. A flash of anger came and went in his eyes and Kelly found herself wanting to make him smile.

"You haven't even kissed me," she pouted.

"I certainly did." He looked pointedly at her breasts.

Remembering how his mouth had felt on her nipples, Kelly flushed.

"I meant on the mouth. Don't you want my mouth?"

"Don't worry, love." He pressed her against the wall and kissed her hungrily. When he finally lifted his head, they both breathed raggedly. Blade grasped her chin and lifted her face to his.

"I have plans for that mouth of yours after dinner."

Once at the restaurant, a waiter led them to a curved booth in a dark corner. Feeling the heat of his body pressed against her, Kelly listened as Blade spoke to Brandon Weston, one of the owners.

"Ethan and I are going to have to put in a few more of these privacy booths." He looked at Kelly's choker pointedly. "More and more people are reserving them." He shook his head and grimaced. "I hope it's not contagious."

Kelly stiffened anxiously when Blade chuckled and shifted to lay a warm hand on the back of her neck, idly playing with the gold chain.

She gasped and closed her eyes against the jolt that went through her. The painful tug on her beaded nipples made her pussy clench. A sharp tug on her hair had her eyes flying open in surprise. She cautiously looked sideways at Blade who scowled at her in warning.

Not knowing what she did wrong, Kelly folded her hands in her lap, and lowered her eyes as she waited for Blade to finish talking to Brandon.

With her eyes partially lowered, she almost missed the look that passed between the two men. When Blade took in her submissive posture, his eyes filled with fierce possession. Those eyes turned to blue chips of ice when he saw the way his friend looked at her.

She heard Blade chuckle and out of the corner of her eye, saw him ruefully shake his head and wondered what Brandon had done to cause it.

"Your waiter is on his way with your wine. After that, well, you know how it works. Have you already ordered?"

"Yes. I spoke to Ethan earlier."

When Blade's hand on her neck began to move again, Kelly lifted her eyes. Her breasts felt swollen, already pushed up high and Kelly feared they would spill over the top of her dress. Her nipples had become so hard and sensitive, she had trouble focusing on anything else. She knew she would have a wet spot on her new dress as moisture continued to seep from her.

Pressing her thighs together, she fought the raging desire and focused on controlling her breathing.

How could she ever get through dinner like this?

"Good," she heard Brandon say. "It's nice to see you both again. Enjoy your dinner."

As Brandon left, the waiter arrived with their wine. Tensely aware of Blade's hand on her neck beneath her hair, Kelly watched Blade taste the wine and nod to the waiter who finished pouring.

When he turned to leave, he paused and Kelly watched in fascination as he pulled a heavy curtain closed behind him.

"I didn't know there was a curtain there," she whispered to Blade. "And why did he only leave one wineglass?"

Now that the waiter had closed the curtain, the booth had become private and more intimate. They couldn't be seen by the other diners and couldn't see them. In fact, they could barely hear them now. The heavy curtain muffled the restaurant noise.

Blade forced her to look up at him. "We only need one glass. You will be fed from my hand. And the curtain is for those of us who want a little privacy."

His eyes hardened. "Speaking of privacy, those hot little noises you make when you're aroused are for my ears only. No one else will be permitted to see or hear you when you come and your moans and gasps of pleasure are mine alone."

When he tugged on the chain attached to her nipples, Kelly moaned and leaned into him.

"That response is mine. If someone else is present, you will lower your eyes, so no one except me sees the way your eyes turn that beautiful deep green when you're aroused. You will not moan or gasp aloud your pleasure in the presence of others." Kelly's head fell back against his hand and she moved closer to brush against him.

"I'll try, Blade. I promise."

"Oh, you'll do more than try, love." His eyes grew hot. "You'll learn control. You'll learn to control your responses, even hold off your orgasm until I allow it."

Taking in her shocked expression, he continued.

"I will push your control beyond its limits over and over."

Kelly could only moan when he tugged on the chain again, pulling it tighter than before. When it turned painful, she automatically lifted her hands to cover her breasts and Blade growled.

"Put your hands down!"

Kelly rushed to obey him. She knew her eyes had widened as she stared at him hungrily. With a last tug, he released the chain and sat back, watching her intently.

"Since you didn't know, I will let that gasp in front of Brandon slide. Further outbursts are considered punishable offenses. Are we clear?"

"Yes, Blade. I'm sorry."

"Good. Now lift up and pull that dress up, so your bare ass is on the leather seat." He took in her stunned expression. "We wouldn't want you to have a wet spot on your new dress, would we?"

He waited until she did as he'd asked before reaching for the bow at her waist.

"Hands behind your back."

Feeling the cool leather on her bare bottom, Kelly couldn't help but feel exposed. Knowing only Blade could see her and that he could put his hand under her dress and easily touch her whenever he wanted made her even hotter.

She watched as he untied the bow from around her waist to where it crossed in the back and used the material to expertly tie her hands behind her.

Kelly's eyes never left Blade's. Through it all, she felt a constant pinch on her nipples, and her hands tied behind her back thrust her breasts out even further. Wearing no panties and her dress lifted, she felt incredibly vulnerable and incredibly aroused.

And except for attaching the chain to her nipples, Blade hadn't even touched her intimately yet.

When she felt his hand skim over her tightly squeezed thighs, she jumped.

"Open these pretty thighs for me."

Kelly parted her thighs several inches, holding her breath in anticipation.

"Wide, Kelly. All the way." Blade pushed his hands between her thighs and forced her legs wide.

"When I tell you to spread your legs, that's how I want them spread. Keep them that way."

Feeling even more exposed, Kelly fought for composure. The cool air brushed over her folds making her slit even wetter.

She watched as Blade sipped his wine as he idly played with the chain. She couldn't keep her eyes from his firm lips and craved them on hers.

To say that Blade had already ruined her for every other man would be an understatement. She never knew she could feel this way and she knew he'd only begun to teach her about herself. She would gladly do whatever he wanted as long as she could experience pleasure like this at his hand.

"Blade, I…" Kelly paused. No. She couldn't tell him of her love just yet.

"What is it, love?"

"May I have some wine?"

"Of course."

With his right hand at the back of her neck holding onto the chain, Blade lifted the wineglass to her lips. The wine tasted delicious, but she didn't care as long as it eased her dry throat.

"I'll be out of town for a few days next week."

She heard Blade's voice as though through a fog and struggled to pay attention. When his words finally penetrated, she felt a sharp stab of disappointment. "Oh."

Blade chuckled and touched his lips tenderly to hers. "I hate being away from you, too, love, especially when I've just begun your training." He tugged on the chain and she felt the sharp pull send sensation all through her body.

"But," his face hardened, "it can't be avoided."

His eyes cleared. "You, however, will have instructions to follow. Next Saturday is your day off, isn't it?"

"Yes." Kelly couldn't help smiling. Did he want to spend the day with her?

"Good. Friday night after work, you will go straight to the spa. Sebastian will take you. They have been instructed on what I want done to you. Afterward, Sebastian will wait to bring you directly back to the club, where you will stay with me until Sunday night. Any questions?"

"So, I should pack for two days?"

"You will pack nothing. Everything you need will be provided. Are we clear?"

"Yes, Blade." Kelly struggled to tamp down her excitement. She couldn't wait to spend the night curled next to Blade.

A light flashed on top of a small box located on the table close to Blade. Next to the light Kelly saw a button that Blade reached over and pushed.

"What's that?" she asked.

"Our appetizers are ready." Blade pushed the hair back from her face. "The waiter won't come in unless I push the button. That way he won't see any more than I want him to see."

"Do you mean that people could be naked in here?" Kelly squeaked.

Blade laughed. "More often than not. Don't worry, love. You're not quite ready for that yet."

Speechless, Kelly watched as the waiter came through the curtain with their appetizers. Did Blade really intend to bring her back here one day and make her sit through dinner completely naked?

How could she handle that?

Her body trembled, unbelievably aroused at what he'd already done to her. She didn't have enough experience at this to be able to control her responses and she knew she certainly didn't have enough to be able to sit here with Blade, completely nude.

Blade said he would teach her control and that she'd better learn or she would be punished.

How would he punish her?

She had no idea, other than a spanking like Clay had threatened her with. Still too new to all this, she didn't have the courage to ask. Already aroused and trying to brace herself for Blade's touch, she didn't need to hear what kind of erotic punishment a man like Blade could think of.

He fed her bites of shrimp and stuffed mushrooms from his plate, offering her sips of wine from his glass, as he asked questions about her work and her brother. They spoke of the town and Kelly asked questions about some of the people she'd only recently met.

"What about Rachel?" Kelly finally asked.

"What about her?"

"Do you like her?"

Blade looked at her quizzically. "Of course I like Rachel. She's a wonderful woman."

"No, I mean like to date."

Blade laughed. "Anyone wanting to date Rachel would have to get through Boone and Chase to do it. While I would be willing to go through them if she and I had that kind of relationship, we don't. Besides, she's so crazy about those two that I doubt if she ever sees anyone else."

"I don't understand. If she's crazy about them, and they're crazy about her, why aren't they together?"

"Boone and Chase have their own set of emotional baggage. Rachel has chased them for months and she's finally come to the conclusion that they don't want her."

"But if they do-"

"Stay out of it, Kelly. They have to work it out themselves."

"But-"

"No, Kelly. Everyone in town knows how they all feel about each other, but Chase and especially Boone stay as far from Rachel as they can. We've all tried to push them together and it only makes it worse."

"It's a shame. Being new here, I guess I have a lot to learn. Ever since I've moved here everyone has been so nice and I want to help whoever I can."

"I, for one, am very thankful that you moved to Desire."

He nuzzled her neck while his hand slid under her dress and teased her clit, maddeningly circling the throbbing nub. His mouth created havoc on her senses. She arched her neck to give him better access which he took full advantage of.

When he stroked lower, circling her opening, she felt it all the way to her toes.

"You're very wet, love."

"I can't help it. It's your fault," she panted. "Oh, Blade, I'm getting the seat all wet."

Blade laughed. "Believe me, love, it's pretty much a given in this booth. It's thoroughly wiped down after each use."

"Oh, God." When Blade's finger pushed inside her, she automatically tightened on it, desperate for release.

A sharp nip on her shoulder made her jump as a deep growl sounded in her ear.

"Spread. Your. Legs."

With a start, Kelly realized she'd closed her thighs on Blade's hand, trying to hold it in place. Quickly she spread them back to their previous position.

"I'm sorry, Blade." She nuzzled him, almost like a puppy, feathering her lips over his strong jaw, feeling his silky hair brush her cheek. "I didn't mean to. I didn't realize…"

When Blade removed his finger, Kelly grew frantic.

"I'm sorry." She kissed his neck and jaw, nuzzling and nipping, reveling in his scent.

When Blade sat back, she moved to follow, but he held her in place with a firm grip on the chain.

"Oh!"

Blade's eyes blazed as he lifted his finger to his mouth and licked her juices from it. "Sweet. I can't wait to put my mouth on that tight pussy and lick that juice from you."

Kelly looked at Blade, shocked. "You want to…?" she swallowed hard, unable to finish.

Blade's eyes sharpened. "Has anyone ever put their mouth on your pussy, love? Has anyone ever sucked on your little clit until you came so hard you screamed yourself hoarse?"

Kelly squirmed in her seat and tried to imagine Blade doing such a thing to her. She shook her head. "No."

A brief flash of something showed in his eyes before he quickly hid it. Wrapping his arms around her, he pulled her across his lap and lowered his mouth to hers.

Flying, Kelly moaned into his mouth. Deep drugging kisses erased all thoughts but him from her mind.

Straightening, he studied her. "I'm going to untie your hands. I want to feel them on me."

"Yes." She desperately wanted to touch him.

Blade freed her hands, letting the material hang and straightened her on his lap. Her hands moved to his shoulders, feeling the strength in them as he adjusted her to his liking, his hands firm on her hips.

She felt giddy which had nothing to do with the small amount of wine she'd consumed. When she saw that the light on the table once again flashed, she placed a hand on each side of Blade's face and leaned in.

"The light's flashing. Our dinner must be ready," she breathed, tracing his lips with her finger.

"So it is."

Kelly continued to caress Blade. She loved having the freedom to be able to touch him like this, aware that his eyes watched hers the entire time. Running her hands through his hair, she pulled his head down and touched her lips to his. She knew next to nothing about kissing. She certainly couldn't equal Blade's expertise, but she put her heart into it, letting her kiss tell him what she didn't dare say out loud.

When Blade ended the kiss, Kelly groaned and unashamedly pressed against him, rubbing her breasts against his wide chest, and delighting in the sensation.

When she tried to lean in again, the hand wrapped in her hair stopped her short. He held her firmly, pulling back until her face lifted, and he could see her features. The action pulled on the chain attached to her nipples.

"We're both going to need our energy. When the waiter comes in this time, I'm going to have my hand on the chain under your hair."

Kelly shivered under his scrutiny. The combined slight pain of his fist tugging her hair and the bite at her nipples had her struggling to pay attention to what he said.

"No matter what, do not let him see any reaction. If you show your arousal, you will face consequences. The look and sounds of your desire belong only to me. You are not permitted to show them to anyone else."

"Blade-" she moaned.

"When we're alone, I want to see and hear everything. You're not permitted to hide it from me."

His eyes glittered darkly. "You will be tested over and over. I want you to learn to release all control only to me. Your tests will become increasingly difficult," he warned. "This is the only time I will ever warn you that I'm about to test you."

He bent and nipped her bottom lip. "You'll always have to be on guard, love."

Kelly trembled as he released her hair and reached under it to grasp the chain. Sitting on his lap, she moaned as he held her right leg over his thigh while moving the other until her left foot wrapped around his leg to rest on his calf. She now sat spread wide on his lap. His hand moved over her thighs and under her dress, and she began to tremble.

"Push the button, Kelly."

Staring into his dark eyes, Kelly struggled to calm down. Could she do this? She had to. She didn't want to disappoint Blade, and she also didn't want to put on a show for the waiter.

When Blade lifted a brow, Kelly knew her time had run out. She stretched her arm out and pushed the button on the box, careful not to move any more than absolutely necessary.

When she felt Blade's thick finger circle her dripping opening, she clenched her hands resting on her thighs into fists. She tensed when she heard the waiter approach and felt Blade give a little warning tug on the chain.

Fire shot through her and she bit her lip to keep from crying out.

"Good girl," she heard him croon at the same time the smiling waiter stepped through the curtain.

Extremely aware of the steadily increasing pull on her nipples, Kelly focused on hiding her response as the waiter served their dinner. If he saw anything strange about serving to two people on a single plate and with only one wineglass, he didn't show it.

Blade had ordered filet mignon and lobster and although the food looked and smelled wonderful, Kelly focused all her attention on remaining quiet and not betraying what Blade did to her.

She kept her eyes lowered and clenched her fists tighter as the pull on her nipples became a sharp erotic pain. When the blunt finger at her slit suddenly pushed into her, Kelly held her breath and bit her lip even harder to keep from crying out.

When would the waiter leave?

A quick glance showed the waiter refilling Blade's wineglass as the two men spoke.

"Kelly, this is Gabriel. Gabriel, this beautiful little spitfire is Kelly. Kelly, say 'hi' to Gabriel."

Kelly heard the amusement in Blade's voice. He enjoyed this! He kept the waiter here longer than necessary just to torture her!

Determined to get him back, Kelly smiled and greeted the young man and shifted on Blade's lap, unobtrusively rubbing her bottom against Blade's erection.

Not by a flicker of an eyelash did Blade betray his arousal or that Kelly's squirming had affected him. His iron control kept any reaction from showing on his face, but Kelly felt him grow and harden beneath her bottom.

Her satisfaction didn't last long, however, when she felt the chain at her neck first tugged, then loosened alternately. Some tugs felt gentle, some much harder, and Kelly never had any idea what the next would be, making it impossible for her to brace for it.

Cursing her stupidity for thinking she could unsettle him, Kelly resigned herself to enduring his retribution.

When the finger inside her began stroking, it momentarily startled her and she had to force herself to remain still. She had already tuned out the conversation Blade had with the waiter, all her attention focused on not showing the effect Blade's actions had on her.

But when she felt Blade's finger curl and stroke the ultra sensitive spot inside her, Kelly knew she wouldn't last.

Oh, no!

Oh God! She would come right here in front of the waiter! She felt the way she kept clenching on his finger but couldn't stop. Lowering her head even further, she squeezed her eyes closed and concentrated on controlling her breathing.

The chain tugged again and held. Blade didn't release it this time and the hard pull on her nipples made them burn. She felt her abdomen tighten and recognized the warning tremors from the night before.

Oh, no! She couldn't stop it!

Bright lights flashed behind her eyes and she felt swept away by the huge wave of release. Every inch of her body felt electrified and at that moment, she wouldn't have cared if she stood naked in the middle of Main Street.

She arched involuntarily and couldn't prevent crying out. Blade immediately smothered her cries with his mouth as his tongue swept through possessively, finally releasing the hold on the chain. His strokes gentled until he slowly withdrew from her dripping depths.

Kelly opened her eyes to find him watching her indulgently.

"I'm sorry," she whispered and glanced over to find the waiter nowhere in sight.

"He's gone," she breathed in relief.

"Of course, love. When I felt how close you were, I thought I'd better get rid of him." He smiled at her tenderly. "The way you respond, I'm surprised you could hold it off as long as you did."

"Oh, Blade," she murmured groggily. "I tried so hard not to. I'm sorry I failed."

"Who said you failed?" He frowned at her. "You did exactly what I wanted you to do. Now tell me, wasn't your orgasm much stronger because you fought against it? Delayed it?"

"Oh, yes!" Kelly's head lolled on his shoulder.

"Did you also learn that no matter how hard you fight it, I can *make* you come, even when you don't want to?"

"Yes, Blade," Kelly answered meekly. She felt as limp as a wet dishrag.

"Good girl. Let me feed you, so we can leave here and go to my playroom. I'm in the mood to play with you." His lips twitched and his eyes glittered fiercely. "With someone sitting on my lap and teasing me by wiggling her ass over my cock, I feel like being a little rough tonight!"

Chapter Five

Blade fed her from his plate between caresses and deep drugging kisses. When he bared her breasts by tugging the snaps free, Kelly basked in the look in his eyes.

Looking down, she saw that her breasts, lifted by her corset, appeared flushed, her nipples hard beads kept that way by the gold rings closed around them. The chain attached to them shone brightly in the candlelit booth. It hung loosely at the moment, but even as Kelly watched, Blade pulled it tighter with the hand at the back of her neck.

As the chain pulled taut, she felt the pull on her nipples all the way to her core, which spasmed with need. She watched, panting when he pulled her nipples upward. They had reddened from the attention they'd already received.

She looked up at Blade to see that he also watched the way the chain pulled her nipples, his eyes hot and possessive as he took in her reaction.

When he lowered his head and used the flat of his tongue on one of the uplifted beads, Kelly gasped and reached for him.

"Put your hands behind your back and keep them there or I'll tie you again," he ordered, his breath hot on her breast.

Dropping her hands, she moved them behind her back and saw how the action lifted her breasts to him even more.

"Mmm, can I expect to find this vanilla flavor all over?"

"Yes!" Kelly bit her lip to keep from crying out as Blade used his teeth on her.

"Then I think we're going to skip dessert until we get to my playroom." His hands stroked her breasts tenderly, his palms rough against their softness and she looked down to see that the powder she'd used made her breasts shimmer in the candlelight.

Blade nipped her. "I have a sudden hunger for vanilla cream."

Kelly groaned, conscious of the diners on the other side of the heavy curtain. Blade used his thumbs on her nipples, rasping them as he held their weight in his palm. She loved the way he combined the rough with the tender, always keeping her guessing.

Adept at both, his touch devastated her senses and when he combined the two, the way he did now, she simply melted.

Carefully snapping her bodice in place, he lifted her effortlessly from his lap and placed her back on the bench next to him before pressing the button on the table.

Sliding a dark glance her way as he refused dessert, Blade signed for the check and escorted Kelly through the restaurant, pausing several times as others greeted them.

She saw the speculative looks when they noticed the choker she wore and several looked pointedly at Blade's matching ring, smiling or winking at her in approval.

It took several minutes before they could leave, and once outside, Blade walked her to his SUV with a hand at her waist. It felt hot and hard and she couldn't help but tremble when she thought about how much pleasure those hot hands gave her.

Even after the orgasm he'd wrung from her in the restaurant, his continued ministrations and heated looks had her aroused again. He kept her body humming to the point that her brain sometimes ceased to function.

When he lifted her into the passenger seat, she gasped, startled when cool leather touched her bottom.

"Oh." Raising startled eyes to Blade, she realized he'd lifted the back of her dress as he'd seated her.

"Get used to it," he warned. "Whenever you're with me, I want that ass and pussy uncovered. When I close the door, spread those legs."

Kelly nodded, dazed, and leaned back against the seat while Blade fastened her seat belt.

She watched as he walked around the front of the truck and couldn't believe he belonged to her.

Well he belonged to her for the next six weeks, anyway.

"Good girl," he murmured when he saw she'd obeyed him, and dropped a hard kiss on her lips before starting the engine.

"Stay that way until we get to the club."

With the club right next door, she followed Blade's instructions easily even though it drove her crazy to be so exposed.

Would tonight be the night he finally took her?

Within minutes Blade pulled into the club's parking lot. Before he could get out, she delayed him with a hand on his arm. "I was jealous when I thought you wanted Rachel."

He leaned over and lifted her face to his. His eyes looked hard in the glare of the parking lot lights. "I agreed not to fuck anyone else for the six weeks I'm with you. That's all. Nothing else is any of your business. All you want from me is sex, right?"

Kelly arched and moaned when he pushed a finger into her soaked opening.

"You wanted the pleasure I can give you. That's what you'll get."

Before Kelly could think of a reply, Blade withdrew from her and got out of the truck. She watched warily as he stalked around the front and opened her door.

She wanted so much more from him than sex. But how could she tell him? She still didn't know if she could handle him, not knowing what he would demand of her.

He would also never believe her.

Resigning herself to keeping her feelings hidden for the next six weeks, Kelly allowed herself to be led inside.

Kelly felt the moisture on her thighs as Blade led her to his playroom. Remembering what he'd said to her, *was it only yesterday*, about being aroused when walking down this hallway, Kelly had to agree.

After experiencing such carnal pleasure, she'd never be able to walk down this hallway and remain unaffected. Kelly watched Blade unlock the door and took a deep breath as she allowed him to usher her inside.

"Strip."

Kelly flinched at Blade's cool command, and remembering how much he hated to wait, she rushed to obey.

He appeared to be in a strange mood tonight and she wasn't sure what caused it. But she knew he wouldn't want to be questioned about it now.

She stepped out of her shoes and handed them to Blade. Her fingers fumbled with the bow on her dress as she hurried to untie it, cursing under her breath when she accidentally knotted it. She struggled with it for several seconds before glancing up anxiously at Blade. She'd already learned to be alert for any signs of displeasure.

She froze when she saw him removing his shirt. Her gaze stayed on his chest as he tossed his shirt onto the bench against the wall. For the first time she saw his naked chest, and her mouth watered at the sight.

Leanly muscled his chest had a smattering of dark hair and she followed the line of hair down past a six pack that proved he stayed in shape. She'd heard somewhere that Doms and their subs needed to stay in shape because of the physical demands of sex in such a lifestyle.

Remembering how effortlessly Blade lifted or adjusted her, she swallowed painfully, worried that she wouldn't be able to keep up.

She continued her journey, following the line of dark hair until it disappeared into his dark pants. The bulge beneath his zipper grew as she watched, and she ached to reach out and touch him.

"Having trouble?"

Her head snapped up at Blade's voice. She thought she saw his lips twitch, but she couldn't be sure.

"I, um, I'm stuck," she admitted, embarrassed. The beautiful and sophisticated women he normally brought here probably never accidentally got themselves stuck because they'd knotted themselves in their dresses.

"Let me help you."

Feeling like an idiot, Kelly held her breath as Blade's gorgeous chest moved closer. She felt his fingers work deftly at the knot, but couldn't tear her eyes from the feast in front of her.

Without thought, Kelly reached out. She just had to touch him. He looked more beautiful than any statue she had ever seen, but the heat radiating from him drew her as no piece of marble ever could. Under her palm, she felt the firmness of muscle beneath the firm hot skin and the tickle of soft springy hair.

When Blade drew in a harsh breath, Kelly jerked her hand away as her eyes flew to his in horror.

"I'm sorry. I didn't, um, I mean, I couldn't, um… I'm sorry."

Lowering her head, she glanced up at him through her lashes. She felt his eyes on her, but kept her head down, not sure if she'd done something wrong again. While at the restaurant, he'd wanted her to touch him. She didn't know if she should touch him here. In Blade's playroom, he unapologetically reinforced his dominance. She'd probably done the wrong thing, touching him, especially in this room without his permission.

Blade looked down at the woman he loved more than life itself, grateful that her eyes had lowered. If not, she would have seen the look of absolute shock on his face when she'd reached out and touched him.

Up until tonight, she'd never initiated physical contact before. He always touched her first. She'd touched his face during dinner, but only after he'd told her to, and she'd only kissed him with those light butterfly kisses when she'd thought she'd made him angry.

Her soft little kisses, asking forgiveness, made him fight his body's reaction as each soft touch of her lips and her desire to appease him brought his cock to full attention.

He couldn't let her know his face tightened fiercely because he'd been grabbing desperately for every ounce of control. His cock had throbbed painfully, needing to be inside her tight, slick sheath and pound into her furiously.

Whether his beloved knew it or not, her submissive nature showed clearly and combined with her defiance, captivated him. He'd never met a woman more suited to the role or more abused by it. He couldn't wait to teach her to embrace her submissive nature. He wanted to show her how her own strength, and teach her that she could be whatever she wanted to be with him.

He would enjoy spoiling her rotten, and when she got too spoiled, well, he would take care of that in a way that would be pleasurable to both of them. He vowed to himself that the only pain she would feel from now on would be erotic pain, the slight pain that only intensified the pleasure.

Jesus, when she'd splayed her dainty hand on his chest, Blade felt as if he'd been touched by a live wire. He smiled to himself. He'd touched and been touched by more women than he could remember, but this little bit of voluptuous curves and shy smiles turned him inside out and tested his iron control with alarming frequency.

It added yet another challenge to the growing number he already faced since finding the woman he wanted to spend the rest of his life with. Knowing she reveled in his dominance, needed it and his strength every bit as much as he needed her softness, he fought to keep his expression cool.

"Did I give you permission to touch me?"

Lifting her chin, he forced her to meet his eyes, seeing both the wariness in her eyes at his expression and the hunger as her eyes kept flicking to his chest.

He finally understood why Nat and Jesse got out of most of their punishments.

She looked absolutely adorable. Still sneaking glances at his chest, she nervously nibbled at her bottom lip. He saw that she'd clenched her hands into fists at her sides as though fighting to keep from touching him. He'd never met a woman so guarded and shy about sex and yet so wonderfully responsive.

She'd been made for him and he would use all of his patience and control to give her whatever she needed to get past her fears regarding intimacy. Only then would she feel free.

Free to accept his love and trust him enough to admit what she felt in return. In the meantime, he'd have to grit his teeth, so she wouldn't realize the effect she had on him. She needed his patience and strength now more than anything, and he would gladly give her both.

"Did I give you permission to touch me?"

Blade's ominous growl made her tremble and she knew she'd made a mistake. Clenching her hands at her sides, she struggled not to touch him. She couldn't stop glancing at his naked chest. She'd never before seen such a magnificent male specimen.

"No. I'm sorry. I didn't think."

Sneaking a peek at him, Kelly continued to bite her lip. He looked so cool and remote she couldn't even guess his thoughts.

"Would you like to touch me, Kelly?"

She looked up at him warily. Was this a test? Not sure what she should say, Kelly decided to go with the truth. He'd spot a lie anyway.

"Yes," she nodded and waited for his reaction.

"Let's take off your dress."

"But the knot," Kelly began, only to look down and see that the knot had been untied and the lengths of material fell from her bodice to the floor between them.

"Oh, you undid it," she muttered inanely and fumbled with the zipper several seconds before finally being able to pull the tab down and allow the dress to puddle at her feet.

"Leave the corset and stockings."

When Blade reached for one of the rings on her nipples, Kelly held her breath.

"You've worn these long enough."

Kelly watched, mesmerized as his big hands loosened the screws from the rings enough to slide them off, removing the chain from around her neck, and tossing it to join the clothing on the bench.

The corset's shelf bra lifted her breasts in a way that a woman would to invite her lover's touch.

Blade accepted the invitation.

When he pinched each of her nipples between a thumb and forefinger, Kelly closed her eyes on a moan. He touched her lightly, but her nipples felt ultra sensitive from the rings and the friction of the dress. His touch devastated her more than ever. He seemed to know just how much she could take, to know exactly how to touch her to bring about the desired effect on her senses.

Obviously experienced, he eyed her coolly as he touched her. With a sinking heart, Kelly wondered how many women he'd brought to his playroom and if she meant anything more to him than just another in a long line of women he'd 'trained'.

"What is it, love?"

Of course, Blade knew something bothered her. With his experience nothing would escape his notice. Knowing he would spot a lie, she blurted out the truth.

"I wondered how many women you've brought to this room. And, um, well if I'm just another number."

Even with her face burning, she forced herself to meet his eyes. Her stomach fluttered when he raised a brow and crossed his arms deliberately over his naked chest. She stifled a groan at the play of muscles, fighting not to stare.

"The number of women I've brought to this room is none of your business."

He studied her for several long seconds before seeming to come to a decision. "I will tell you this, though. This room is my *personal* playroom, not the club playroom. I didn't realize that you wanted to be more than just a number. You just want to see if you can have sex again, give up control, right?"

More than anything, Kelly wanted to blurt out the truth, to tell Blade she wanted him and loved him enough to give herself over to him to see if she could be the kind of woman he'd need. But she couldn't. She still didn't know if she would be able to have sex with him, knowing he would want to dominate her.

They hadn't even had sex yet! How could she know?

She couldn't deal with him being unfulfilled, and she didn't know if she could fulfill him.

Lowering her eyes, so he couldn't see the lie in them, she nodded. "Right."

An idea occurred to her. "Blade, can I ask you for a favor?"

She couldn't help but wince at Blade's frown.

"You do know that this room is not the place to get into these little talks, don't you?"

"I know, but this is important."

When he just stood there with his arms folded over his chest and stared at her, she struggled not to flinch.

"What is it, Kelly?"

"I want you to, um, make sure that you, I mean, I do everything you like before the six weeks are over." Kelly felt her face burn, but raised her chin defiantly. "I want to make sure that I can take you at your most demanding."

Forcing herself to remain still under his searching look, Kelly waited breathlessly for his answer. She flinched when he chuckled.

"Do you really think you'll be able to take it? Within six weeks?" Blade moved closer and grasped her chin, his voice a soft amused rumble. "Do you really believe you'll be able to satisfy my darkest, most extreme desires without using your safe word?"

He wanted to scare her! He practically dared her to use her safe word. Her newfound confidence wouldn't let her back down.

"Yes!" She had to. Loving Blade as she did, she knew she would at least have to try. Wondering what she would experience filled her with both fear and need, and made her add, "I'll even give up my safe word."

Blade grinned, clearly enjoying this.

The rat.

"Oh, no, you won't. Trust me, love. You'll be screaming it at the top of your lungs before the six weeks are over."

He really wanted to see if she would go through with this, didn't he? She could do this. She'd show him he couldn't scare her.

Well, he scared the hell out of her but she wouldn't let him know it.

He'd know, damn it! Of course he'd know, but she wouldn't let it get the best of her.

Besides, she wanted the chance to shake that damned control of his. Then he would see that she perfectly suited him.

"No. I won't."

"We'll see. Now, not another word from you unless I ask you a question." He reached for her hands and placed them on his chest.

"You said you wanted to touch me. Go ahead."

Kelly needed no further encouragement. She desperately wanted to explore the magnificent sight before her. She couldn't see an ounce of fat anywhere on him. All lean muscle, and darkly smooth, he took her breath away. Her eyes feasted on him as her hands roamed freely, eager to explore, as excited as a child on a new playground.

Her playground, she thought greedily, wanting it all to herself.

When she touched her fingers to hard male nipples, she glanced up. Other than a slight tightening of his jaw, he showed no reaction. Leaning forward, she touched her tongue to one and felt him shudder. He tasted like sin, slightly salty and dangerously erotic. She felt him shudder when she did it again.

Good. She wanted to shake him and vowed that before her six weeks ended, she'd learn how to make him lose control completely. Already he chipped at hers. His scent wrapped around her filling her with hunger.

Running her hands over his biceps, she moved around him, trailing her lips over his back, feeling the muscles bunch and shift where she touched. When his hand circled her wrist and pulled her back around in front of him, Kelly continued kissing and nibbling, using her tongue to taste him.

God, he tasted so good! He tasted hot and spicy and she felt herself getting even wetter as she responded to the scent and taste of her lover.

Bending slightly, she used her hands and mouth to explore his stomach and abdomen. She moved lower until she reached his belt buckle and looked up at him questioningly.

She needed him inside her.

"Do you want my cock, love?"

"Oh, yes!" Kelly reached for his belt buckle.

"Hands at your sides!"

Startled, she released him and lowered her hands, frowning in puzzlement.

"I didn't give you permission to undo my trousers. Next time, wait until you're told."

When she opened her mouth to speak, Blade raised a dark brow. "I didn't ask you anything."

Snapping her mouth closed, Kelly watched him warily. She would go crazy with wanting if he didn't hurry up and do something soon.

Glancing down at the impressive tenting below his belt buckle, she unconsciously licked her lips.

"That's right, love. Get those lips nice and wet. I'm going to enjoy fucking that hot little mouth of yours."

Glancing up, she saw that his features had hardened into a mask of complete dominance, raw power, and fierce arousal.

Her eyes widened as her entire body reacted. Her breasts swelled and ached to be touched. Her slit dripped even more and her insides clenched when her clit began to throb. Even her bottom tingled!

There he is!, her body seemed to scream at her. This is the man who controls your body. *This* is your body's master!

A shuddering breath escaped as Kelly realized just how completely she lost herself in him, caring about nothing more than Blade's scent, his touch, the sound of his voice as he drowned her in need.

She knew Blade couldn't help but notice her reaction. She couldn't have hidden it from him if her life depended on it.

Other than a slight narrowing of his eyes and a satisfied curl of his lips, his expression never changed.

"I'm going to take that sweet mouth of yours tonight," he murmured lowly. "You're going to take me all the way to your throat and suck me as I stroke in and out of that hot mouth."

Kelly trembled with both fear and excitement. She couldn't wait to taste him, to finally be able to touch and please him, but she knew from being forced to endure Simon in such a way, choking and gagging with tears running down her face as she fought to merely get through it, that pleasing Blade in this way may be more than she could handle.

Not surprised that he'd noted her anxiety, he asked, "What's wrong, love?"

"I don't know how," she admitted, feeling once again like a stupid twit. "Simon forced me, but…will you teach me?"

"Of course, love. We'll go slowly in all things and I will teach you everything you need to learn."

She sighed in relief at his tenderness. Her relief didn't last, however, when he continued.

"First, I need to continue to work on loosening those tight muscles in your ass. Come with me."

Guided across the room with a hand on her back, Kelly trembled and looked on nervously as Blade gestured toward a shelf.

"Those are your butt plugs."

"Mine?"

"Yes. Quiet. It wasn't a question. I bought them just for you. As you can see, there are five of them in varying sizes, from this," he picked up the smallest, which to her seemed pretty big, "to this."

Kelly felt a frisson of fear as she looked at the one on the right, the largest, as Blade pointed to it.

"This one is almost as wide as my cock." He grinned evilly. "By the time your tight little ass adjusts to this one, you should be able to take my cock without too much trouble."

He paused. "Don't worry, love. You love the sharp bite of pain when I enter your ass and the burn of the muscles being stretched. Imagine how good it's going to feel when I fuck that ass."

He reached for a tube. "Tonight, however, I'm taking your mouth, but I want the first plug imbedded in your bottom when I do it."

Kelly felt her slit weep even more moisture. She couldn't believe how much she wanted all the things he threatened to do to her. She loved turning herself over to him this way, needing his strength, his experience, his command of both his body and hers.

He led her to the end of the padded table.

"Bend over."

His cool command sent a shiver straight through her. She slowly bent over the end of the table, moaning when her nipples touched the cool leather surface.

"Do you need to be restrained?"

"No. Yes. I don't know. Please, whatever you want."

"Good girl. I won't strap you down this time. Next weekend, though, I'm going to spend a lot more time stretching your ass and I'll have to restrain you for that."

Kelly groaned and she briefly wondered if Blade was testing her. She felt another flood of moisture and a thick finger pressing into her pussy.

"You like that, I see. The rougher and more demanding I get, the more aroused you become. I might have to work harder before you say your safe word."

"No. I won't say it!"

"We'll see, love. Now, give your ass to me. Spread those luscious cheeks and show me what belongs to me."

Kelly didn't even try to contain the tremors that ran through her. Reaching down, she parted her bottom cheeks, feeling more exposed than she'd ever felt in her life. Blade's harsh and wicked demands thrilled her. She had trouble coping with the fact that she reveled in it, needed it, and needed him. She obeyed him, losing all inhibitions, needing to give him whatever he wanted from her because each time she did, he took her higher, gave her more.

A thick finger, cool with lube touched her anus and her trembling increased.

"How pretty. Is this mine?"

"Oh, God, yes!"

"Whenever I want it, you will bend over and give it to me?"

"Yes!"

"I can fill it anytime I want?"

"Yes, please! It's yours!"

With that a slick finger pushed inside her and Kelly shook.

"How does that feel, love?" He began to stroke slowly inside her.

When she didn't answer right away, she felt a sharp slap on her bottom.

"Answer me!"

"Oh! I feel, I feel, full and exposed." She couldn't stop clenching on his finger. "And naughty."

"You are naughty, love, just the way I like you. You're very tight here. This little opening will have to be stretched quite a bit."

"Oh God!"

She heard Blade chuckle as another finger circled her pussy entrance.

"You like being a naughty girl, don't you, love? The naughtier you get, the wetter you become. Your pussy is soaked."

When both fingers pulled abruptly from her, Kelly wiggled, empty and needy.

Another sharp slap landed on her bottom and she froze.

"Be still. You will not move again while I shove this plug into your ass. Release your bottom and put your hands above your head."

Kelly hurried to obey him, feeling the warmth on her bottom where he'd slapped her spread to her pussy and clit. Her nipples rasped against the table as she raised her arms above her head. Her clit throbbed painfully and she felt the tingles of her approaching orgasm.

Almost mindless with need, Kelly sucked in a breath when she felt her bottom cheeks being parted. She forced herself to remain still when she felt more of the slippery lube being worked into her, then the cool hardness of the plug being slowly pushed past the tight ring of muscle.

The sharp bite of pain and the slow steady burn in her anus made her toes curl as she clenched on the plug greedily. It took a moment to realize the harsh panting moans she heard came from her.

"Relax those muscles, love. I need to push this deep inside you."

The combination of the burn and Blade's words made her clit throb even more painfully and with no other thought but easing her torment, Kelly used her hands to grip the table edge and rock her body. The friction of the leather covered table on her clit sent her over the edge into a screaming climax.

Feeling the rest of the plug being shoved to the hilt inside her only increased her pleasure. Wave after wave of ecstasy washed over her as she continued to rock her body, her movements easing with her orgasm. She breathed heavily when she finally released her grip on the table.

Several seconds passed before Kelly became aware of an ominous silence in the room.

Oh, no! What had she done? She wasn't supposed to come until he allowed it!

Damp with perspiration and weak from the incredible orgasm she'd just had, Kelly fought to catch her breath. The plug in her bottom felt much larger than it had looked in Blade's hand. She felt the muscles holding it clench as the plug awakened nerve endings in a way that felt unfamiliar to her, creating a new hunger that disconcerted her.

She needed Blade. She needed to hear his voice, feel his touch. Whether a cool command, a growl, or a low and soothing croon, she needed his voice, his touch to center her.

Blinking at the sting of tears, Kelly wondered fearfully what Blade thought. The women he'd brought here in the past had probably never lost control the way she had. He probably thought her immature, unable to get out of her dress without a struggle and losing control the way she just had.

More tears fell, dripping onto the table beneath her. Afraid of making yet another mistake, she didn't move or speak, fearfully waiting for Blade's reaction.

Oh, please don't let this be the end of their agreement. She would die if he told her it was over.

"I should walk away from you right now."

"Please, no!" Kelly struggled to remain still when she wanted to jump up from her position bent over the table and run to him, throw herself in his arms and beg forgiveness.

When Blade moved into her peripheral vision and stroked a hand slowly, deliberately from her buttocks and up her spine, tears of relief filled her eyes. She needed this, needed the connection. He seemed to know it and she drew a shuddering breath, grateful that once again, he gave her what she needed.

"Why should I waste my time trying to train such an undisciplined submissive?" he asked her coolly. "Only a few minutes ago, you assured me that you can take whatever I dish out and almost immediately have the audacity to bring yourself to orgasm, deliberately disobeying me, in my presence and in the room that more than anywhere else, I demand total obedience and submission from you."

The ice in his voice froze her. When he lifted her trembling form off the table to stand in front of him, she looked up to see the same cold look in his eyes.

She wiped at the tear trickling down her face and stared up at him blinking furiously. "I'm so sorry. I just couldn't stand it anymore."

It seemed impossible, but his eyes became even colder.

"Now, you're going to tell me how much you can take? *I* decide what you can and cannot take. Not you. Remember?"

Reaching out, Kelly gripped his arms. "Please give me another chance. I'm really sorry. It won't happen again."

She shrugged her shoulders helplessly. "All of this is still new to me. I'm trying, Blade. Honest. Please don't give up on me. Give me another chance."

When Blade looked down pointedly at where her hands gripped his arms and raised a brow, Kelly immediately dropped her hands to her sides.

Damn, she'd messed up again.

Blade stared at her intently for what seemed like hours, stretching her nerves to the breaking point. Just when she thought she couldn't stand another second, he spoke, his words both thrilling and terrifying.

"You do know that what you did demands disciplinary action, don't you?"

Kelly gulped nervously and nodded. "Yes, I know. I'm sorry for what I did and I accept whatever punishment you think I deserve."

She breathed a sigh of relief when Blade nodded in satisfaction, but his next words took her breath away.

"Punishment can come in all forms. Since this is your first real punishment, I'll go easy. You will strip off the corset and stockings and lay yourself over my lap. I will spank you until your ass is red and hot and I think you've been punished enough. Since this is your first time, I will use my hand instead of the paddle or whip."

Kelly felt her eyes widen and unconsciously tightened her butt cheeks, which in turn made the plug inside her feel even larger. Her trembling increased as Blade continued.

"You will have the plug remain inside you the entire time and you will keep your legs spread. When I'm finished, you will get on your knees with your hands behind your back. I'm going to fuck that mouth nice and slowly, *or* rough and demandingly." He smiled at her coldly. "It depends on how well you take your spanking."

Kelly knew she would do whatever she had to do to accept his punishment better than anyone ever had. His words sent spikes of pure lust through her, arousing her again, forcing her to admit to herself that she craved this. Starved for the pleasure she knew only Blade could give her, she vowed to give him what he expected from her.

"Afterward," he continued darkly, "you will bend over that table again where I will remove the plug inside you and exchange it for a larger one, which you will wear until tomorrow morning. Do you understand?"

"Yes, Blade," Kelly moaned, not sure if she could stand much more.

"Then you will lie on the table with your legs spread, holding yourself open to me. I want my vanilla cream."

"Oh, yes, Blade. Anything!"

"While my mouth is on you, you will not come."

"W-what?" Kelly stuttered, not believing she'd heard him correctly.

"You heard me. You can only come with my permission. You've already taken your pleasure, remember?"

"Oh, no! I'll never make it!" Already aroused, she knew it would only get worse. She couldn't wait to take his hard length into her mouth and give him pleasure, show him how much she wanted to please him. Her pussy wept just thinking about it.

Once he put his mouth on her, she knew she couldn't stop an orgasm from overtaking her.

Kelly watched Blade move away from her and retrieve a chair, placing it several feet away. Seating himself, he patted his thigh and looked over at her expectantly.

Blade watched the fear and excitement war for supremacy on Kelly's face as she quickly undressed and glided toward him. He knew she had to be nervous about her spanking, but now she worried more about her inability to hold off her orgasm.

His cock jumped when Kelly draped her naked form over his lap. With a hand between her thighs, he spread her legs the way he wanted them.

He pushed against the butt plug and heard her gasp. Shaking his head, he smiled. He couldn't believe how she responded when he focused his attention on her ass. He'd known she'd been close, but had assumed that with a history like hers, she would have been pulled from the edge when he pressed the plug into her.

Instead it pushed her over.

He could have easily stopped her when she'd rubbed herself against the table, but he wanted her to connect the feeling of anal play with pleasure instead of fear and pain.

He'd stood there, astounded once again by her sensuality. He'd finally found his perfect partner. Her complete surrender to him spurred his dominate nature to even greater heights. She challenged him on so many levels, he would have to spend the rest of his life meeting them. His need for her and his pleasure with her continued to grow and he couldn't wait until he felt those sweet lips wrapped tightly around his cock.

Forcing himself to go slowly with her would kill him. It also rewarded him in ways he couldn't have imagined.

Holding her firmly in place with a hand on her back, he ran his hand lovingly over the curves of her ass, smiling to himself as she shivered. Mesmerized by the sight of his dark hand over her pale, rounded bottom, Blade couldn't help imagining working his cock between those cheeks.

His cock jumped again. He had to stop thinking about that or he would come in his trousers before he even fucked her mouth.

Not a great precedent for a Dom to set.

First things first. The time had come to see how his hand would look against her very *red* ass.

Kelly couldn't stop shaking. She could only imagine what she looked like splayed over Blade's lap. He'd spread her legs, and she knew he could see the moisture dripping from her, could probably feel it soaking his pant leg.

The hands holding her in place felt hot and hard, and she knew she'd never be able to move. Another caress on her bottom made her trembling increase.

Why didn't he hurry up and get it over with? She wanted to scream at him to hurry, but she didn't want to get into any further trouble.

When the first hard slap landed, she jerked and would have fallen off Blade's lap if he hadn't been holding her in place. The slap stung more than she'd been prepared for and she swallowed a whimper.

"You're not going to make it through this without making a sound, love. Don't try to hide it from me. You'll only earn yourself more."

"I thought you wanted me to be quiet."

"No, love. I said no talking. I want to hear the rest, all your little sounds."

Blade smoothed a hand over the cheek he'd just slapped. The warmth of his hand heated the area even more. The heat began to spread.

Slap.

A startled cry escaped before she could prevent it.

The second slap heated her other cheek and when Blade rubbed the spot, the heat again began to spread. He continued spanking her, sometimes several sharp slaps in rapid succession, sometimes spaced out, several long moments between them.

The heat had spread all over and it wasn't long before Kelly was wiggling on Blade's lap.

Her cries and moans filled the room and she found herself raising her bottom into Blade's hand. She didn't care. Panting and breathless, her body damp from exertion, it was several moments before she realized her punishment had ended.

Instead, he now crooned to her, praising her as he continued to stroke her heated bottom.

"Good girl. You handled that very well, love. I'm very proud of you."

Kelly lay panting and moaning over Blade's lap. She'd never been over anyone's lap before and couldn't quite assimilate the erotic feel of it. She felt very feminine and vulnerable, but more aware of her body and sexuality than ever before.

She felt very helpless and exposed as she always did with Blade, but more desired than she'd ever felt. He made her feel cherished, as if she'd become the most important person in the world to him.

Even when he spanked her.

He seemed to know her, both her body and her mind better than she did, and no matter what he demanded of her, no matter what he did to her, her pleasure appeared to be his ultimate goal.

She'd already had several orgasms at his hand, but he hadn't yet come with her. Lying over his lap, her body vibrating with need, she felt Blade's hand caressing her bottom, spreading the heat, and wanted desperately to give him the kind of pleasure he'd given her.

"You have a magnificent ass, love. It's a nice shade of pink and *very* warm."

Kelly felt two of his fingers push their way inside her quivering wetness, and arched to give him better access.

"Good girl," he crooned, and she warmed at his praise. "You liked your spanking, didn't you, love?"

Kelly's moaned, yes, preceded more moans of pleasure as he stroked his fingers in and out of her. She cried out in distress when he removed them.

"I hope you're not going to make me do this often, love. I would much prefer spending my time enjoying your body in other ways, but if I need to punish you, I will. This was only a minor one, being your first, and you handled it well."

With a last caress on her bottom, Blade helped her to stand. His grip steadied her when she swayed. When he lifted a hand to cup her cheek, she automatically curled her face into it and closed her eyes.

He always knew what she needed.

She needed these soothing caresses, letting her know that even though she'd disappointed him earlier, he still desired and forgave her.

It made her want him even more. Even if he didn't love her, she could feel how much he wanted her. He made her feel special, something no man had ever made her feel before.

"Now I'm going to take that hot little mouth of yours."

Kelly watched, practically drooling, as Blade finished undressing. When he finally stood before her completely naked, she looked at his rock hard erection in awe.

Her trembles turned into shakes. Blade cock looked *huge*, much larger than Simon's. Remembering the pain Simon had caused, she could only imagine the pain she'd feel when Blade pushed that *beast* inside her.

Her fear must have shown on her face because Blade moved closer and lifted her gaze from his formidable length. His eyes had softened with understanding.

"It's all about trust, love. I will guide you in all things and I've already promised you that I'll go slowly."

Kelly nodded shakily. Blade had been so patient with her. He probably didn't have women who blew hot and cold the way she did. One minute she shook with arousal, the next she shuddered in fear.

He knew it, of course. He spun her around, his erection pressing against her back, tilting her head, so he could nibble on the ultra sensitive spot between her neck and shoulder. She closed her eyes as electricity shot through her.

He lifted her arms to circle his neck as his mouth continued its journey. Her hands gripped him, tangling in his silky hair as her head fell back against his shoulder. He cupped her breasts, pinching her nipples lightly.

She responded immediately and automatically. Arching, she pressed her breasts more firmly against his palms and tilted her head to give him better access.

"Don't you dare come."

The growl in her ear made her moan, then whimper when his hand left her breasts to travel down her stomach, over her mound and beyond. When devious fingers slipped between her folds, she gasped and tightened her hold on him.

It didn't take long before Kelly felt the now familiar tingle signifying her impending orgasm. Fighting it with everything she had, she bit her lip and tried to think of anything, *anything,* that would stop it.

She couldn't silence the gasping cries of distress as she fought it, needing to show Blade she could be what he wanted, take what he could give her.

Just when she thought the next flick of his finger would push her over the edge, Blade stopped and slowly withdrew his hand.

Somehow he'd known she needed only one more stroke to explode.

When he untangled her hands from his neck and turned her to face him, she saw that his face had tightened with need.

"On your knees."

The softly spoken command went to her head like wine. Nothing else mattered. She only thought of Blade and the white hot pleasure he gave her.

Without hesitation, she dropped to her knees in front of him and gripped his thighs. The muscles under her hands felt thick and rock hard.

The steely length between them interested her even more.

She couldn't take her eyes from it, her breath quickening when Blade gripped his cock behind the large purplish head with one hand and the back of her head with the other.

"Hands behind your back!"

She hurried to obey, having forgotten that part.

"Open your mouth, Kelly."

Thoughts of Simon's violence intruded and Kelly felt her eyes prick with tears as she opened her mouth and braced for the onslaught. Forced to open her mouth wider to accommodate the large head, she tensed, expecting him to shove his length into her mouth forcefully.

When he stopped with only the head of his cock in her mouth, she slowly relaxed her jaw.

"Let me feel that hot little tongue on my cock. Lick me, Kelly."

She had no experience with pleasing a man with her mouth other than trying not to gag as Simon shoved to her throat. Intrigued now, Kelly wanted more than anything to please him. Swiping her tongue tentatively over the tip, Kelly tasted the drops that had escaped.

Her first taste of her lover had her hands clenching into fists. He tasted slightly salty and exotic, hot and dark and without thought, she used her tongue to dart into his opening to taste more. She sucked on him between little licks, his taste addictive.

Hearing Blade's groan of encouragement, she grew even hotter. The growl in his voice as he praised her and the harshness of his breathing made her greedy. She took him further and further into her mouth, sucking gently and using her tongue, eager to please him but also because her own hunger continued to grow.

When she swept the underside, beneath the plum sized head, she heard him groan and felt his hands tighten in her hair. Elated that she'd done something that pleased him, she did it again.

And again.

Tasting more of the exotic saltiness, she sucked him deeper, wanting all of him.

"That's it, love," he groaned. "I love the feel of that soft little tongue on my cock. Yes, keep taking me deeper. Good girl."

In her enthusiasm, Kelly pulled him deeper. She accidentally took him too far and gagged, panicking as she fought to breathe. But, even now his control came through.

"Easy, love." He pulled back slightly and stroked her cheek. "Breathe through your nose. Good girl."

Kelly did as he directed, thankful for his calm instruction. It helped keep her fear at bay. When he pulled her arm forward and took one of her hands in his, cupping it around his tight sack, she curled her hand around it, softly exploring.

Hearing the sharp intake of breath and the way his hard length jumped inside her mouth, Kelly sucked him harder, using her tongue on the spot she'd discovered earlier as she continued stroking his sack. He pulled her other hand forward and placed it around the base of his cock. With his hand over hers, he taught her the rhythm he liked.

"That's good, love. Now keep your hand there and take me deeper. Your hand will keep you from taking me too far."

Hungry for his taste and needing to hear the sounds that told her she gave him pleasure, Kelly drew him in.

Breathing through her nose the way he'd taught her, she took him to the back of her throat, all the while stroking the base of his thick shaft, and fondling the sack below.

She loved how he swelled on her tongue, the way his hips started to move, thrusting shallowly into her mouth. Now prepared for the depth of the thrusts, Kelly no longer panicked and all her thoughts centered on pleasing Blade.

"Swallow on me."

When she did as he asked, he groaned.

"When I come, swallow all of it."

With a last thrust, she felt Blade's hot seed spurt down her throat. She swallowed repeatedly, her pussy clenching as his cock pulsed. When he slid from her mouth, she moved her hands to his quivering thighs, caressing tenderly as she lovingly licked him clean.

When he bent and lifted her, her legs automatically wrapped around his waist and she nuzzled his neck. His hands on her bottom held her firmly and the plug inside her shifted with every step he took.

When Blade placed her bottom on the edge of the table, the plug pushed deeper into her and she clung weakly to him.

He smothered her gasp as his mouth took possession of hers. More devastating than ever, he swept his tongue through the dark recesses as though he owned it. Owned her. She could do nothing but part her lips and allow him the freedom to take what he wanted. Her tongue chased his in an erotic dance as she pursued him.

When he lifted his head, she saw the fierce satisfaction on his face.

"You have the most incredible mouth."

Smiling her own satisfaction, she nuzzled his chest. "I'm glad I could give you pleasure. Thank you for being so patient with me and for teaching me."

"There are many things I'd like to teach you, love." A wicked grin lit his face.

He lifted her to her feet and turned her to once again face the table. Fisting her hair in his hand, he pulled it aside, exposing her sensitive neck to his mouth. Nuzzling and biting her, he made her shiver and sent jolts of lust through her.

"Let's stretch that ass a little more," he whispered darkly as his hands covered her breasts.

"Oh God," she whimpered, totally lost in need for Blade and what he made her feel. He'd taken her over and kept her too aroused to feel anything except the need to give him whatever he wanted, the need to submit to his demands, knowing that by doing so, he would continue taking her higher.

His hands gripped her gently, but firmly as he bent her once again over the padded table. "I'm going to restrain you this time, love," Blade told her and a light slap on her bottom made her jump.

"I can't have you pleasuring yourself again, now, can I?"

Kelly couldn't stifle her moan when Blade pulled her hands above her head and secured them to the cuffs at the top of the table. She loved being so helpless to his demands!

She shivered when he trailed his fingers down her back as he moved down the length of the table. The cheeks of her bottom tightened involuntarily when his fingers moved down her cleft toward where the plug invaded her.

Once again between her thighs, his fingers moved over her bottom and to the sensitive area on the inside of her thighs.

She wiggled shamelessly, needing him to touch her higher, her dripping pussy and throbbing clit demanding attention.

She jumped as a sharp slap landed on each cheek.

"I see I'll always have to restrain you when I need you to be still."

Blade's tone aroused her even more. She felt a strap tighten over first one thigh and then the other before being spread far apart. She heard a click and wiggled again, but couldn't move. She groaned harshly as Blade continued to stroke closer and closer to her center, feeling her body burn for him.

She gasped when he gripped the base of the plug and slowly, teasingly withdrew it from her anus. Gripping it, she tried desperately to keep it from being withdrawn. Struggling, she tried to move on it. She mewed in frustration, not having the ability to move enough to satisfy her needs.

When she heard Blade's dark laugh, she wanted to hit him.

"Poor baby. You can't move enough to fuck your ass with the plug, can you?"

He jerked the plug out of her, making her cry out in frustration and leaving her clenching uselessly at the emptiness in her bottom.

Her struggles continued and she knew he watched, but had become so aroused she no longer cared. She begged and pleaded, her hands gripping the top of the table until her knuckles turned white.

"Do you need a bigger plug in your bottom, love?"

"Yes! No! I don't know."

It didn't even bother her when he chuckled again. He could laugh all he wanted as long as he *did* something to relieve this horrible ache.

When she felt the tip of the plug press against her, she froze.

"It would seem the best way of controlling you is with your ass, either spanking it or filling it."

He began to press the plug into her. "It makes me anxious to find out how good you'll be when I fuck it."

She knew, *knew,* he could tell what his words did to her, but she couldn't control the dark thrill that shot through her at his threat.

He stroked the large plug in and out of her, fucking her ass with it and she couldn't prevent from lifting, as much as she could, into his thrusts, crying out in need as the burn of her body stretching consumed her.

By the time the new plug pressed completely inside her, she panted frantically, the tremors shaking her body with renewed vigor.

When Blade undid her restraints and turned her, she collapsed in his arms. He held her against him, stroking her tenderly before laying her back on the table.

"Now I want my dessert." He scowled at her. "Remember, you don't come without my permission. Lie back, so I can have my vanilla cream."

"Oh, God!"

As soon as she lay back, Blade lowered his mouth to her dripping wetness. The first swipe of his tongue on her slit had her crying out. Already on the edge, she knew she would never last.

The hands on her thighs tightened, effectively holding her in place.

"Mmmm, I love my treat."

Another swipe made her writhe. He seemed intent on using his mouth to learn every part of her delicate folds. When he speared his tongue inside her, Kelly would have arched off the table if he hadn't held her.

"No, please. I can't stop it." Twisting her head from side to side, she fought his onslaught.

"Don't you dare come!"

She felt his hot breath on her clit as he growled the demand. Her thighs shook, her toes curled and she knew she couldn't last much longer.

When Blade lifted his head and straightened, Kelly fought to catch her breath, taking in great gulps of air as she struggled to pull back from the edge.

"Thankyouthankyouthankyou."

Kelly kept repeating the words over and over as she tried to cool down, pulling herself from where she hung from her fingertips on the edge.

"What are you thanking me for, love?

Kelly felt every muscle in her body quiver as Blade looked down at her from the end of the table.

"For stopping. I couldn't hold it back any more. You told me not to come and I was afraid I wasn't going to make it."

Blade smiled at her indulgently. "You're *not* going to make it. I just paused to watch your face. Now I'm going to put my mouth on your throbbing little clit and suck it the way you sucked my cock."

"No, Blade. I'll come," she whispered frantically.

"Yes, love. You will."

As his head lowered, she closed her eyes and braced herself.

"Say my name!"

She heard Blade's growled demand a second before his tongue touched her clit.

"Blade!"

His tongue touched and retreated, almost, but not quite making her go over.

"BladeBladeBladeBlade," she whimpered over and over until suddenly he closed his lips around her hard nub and sucked.

Hard.

"Blaaaaaaade!"

Her body bucked, shaking hard as the pleasure went on and on. She couldn't stop screaming his name over and over.

Not until she'd become hoarse from screaming his name did he lift his head. She felt as if her bones had melted as she lay panting on the table.

Blade ran his hands over her. Before long before she felt her trembling body come alive again. She soon became hungry for him, ready to do whatever he wanted. It appeared she could never have enough of him.

How did he do this to her?

"I already fucked that hot little mouth. Now I'm going to fuck your tight pussy."

"Yes, Blade. Please take me!"

His eyes glittered darkly, his face a mask of tension and need, a look that made her heart race.

"Open yourself. Show me what belongs to me," he demanded roughly.

Her hands trembled as she reached down to part her folds, exposing her pussy and clit to his heated gaze. His eyes held hers as he stroked all that she'd exposed to him.

"Is this mine? Does all of this belong to me?"

"Yes!" Kelly cried out, needing to give him everything.

"This pussy is mine?"

Kelly moaned when he pushed a blunt finger into her too sensitive opening.

"Yes," she panted, moving on his finger.

When she felt him start to withdraw, she whimpered, and then gasped as he used it to circle her clit.

"Does this little red clit belong to me? Is it mine to stroke, to tease, to suck into my mouth whenever I want it?"

"Yes, anything."

The fierce expression on Blade's face held her spellbound.

Raw desire, possession, satisfaction and something else, a tenderness that made her heart jump warred on his features but like before, it only lasting a second before being shuttered.

She heard the rip of foil and looked down to see him roll on a condom.

Then her mind went blank as he began to push into her. She caught her breath as her body struggled to accept him. With the plug inside her, she didn't think it was possible.

"So fucking tight. So hot."

Blade's deep growl sent a shiver of elation and a little fear through her and she tensed as the large head passed the threshold.

"Aaahhh, no love. Don't tense up. Easy, love."

She stared at him, watching his struggle for control, grateful that he could rein it in enough that he didn't plunge into her.

It cost him, though. His face became a mask of anguish, his eyes closed, his jaw tight as sweat poured off him. He looked tortured and even more beautiful to her than ever.

Fear that his tenuous hold on his control would shatter, she held herself still. Amazed that she could bring him to this point filled her with elation and she unconsciously relaxed her inner muscles.

"That's it, love. Let me inside you."

She'd never been this full, hadn't known she could stretch like this. She felt the muscles in her pussy burn with a delicious heat as he worked his cock into her. He stroked shallowly at first, then deeper with each thrust, hitting that ultra sensitive spot inside.

"Oooohh, Blade. I can't stop it."

"Come, love. Come. For. Me."

Each word followed a devastating stroke and soon she had no choice but to obey him. Her body bowed, the strong hands gripping her hips holding her in place as nerve endings tingled and sparked, making her shudder as she once again screamed his name.

She dimly heard Blade's deep growl as he slammed into her fully, the deep penetration stealing her breath. Her back arched, lifting her breasts high as Blade's thick heat slammed into her. Another orgasm crashed over her, sending her spiraling into white hot ecstasy.

Blade sounded as though in agony, groaning hoarsely, his breathing labored before a long, deep roar rumbled from his chest.

Only harsh breathing could be heard as they both struggled to recover. Kelly realized dimly that tears ran down her face.

Blade leaned over her, his cheek pressed against her breast. When he raised his head, the deep satisfaction on his face changed to horror.

"Oh, God. Kelly, love, did I hurt you?"

The concern and caring on his face undid her. Unable to speak, she shook her head as sobs overtook her. When she felt his strong arms go around her, felt herself cradled against his chest, Kelly clung.

He straightened, holding her against him, his lips in her hair, crooning to her. She had no idea what he said, but eventually quieted, embarrassed by her outburst.

He sat in the same chair he'd used for her spanking, her legs on either side of his narrow hips and raised his hands to her face. Using his thumb to wipe a stray tear from her cheek, he forced her gaze to his.

"Are you okay, love?"

She nodded shakily. "I'm sorry," she sniffed. "I don't know what happened."

He lowered his head, taking her lips hungrily, pulling her tightly against his chest as though trying to absorb her into his body.

When he lifted his head to stare down at her, she blinked, trying to clear her head. His sharp gaze stayed steady on her and she wondered what he saw that made his lips twitch in amusement.

"You really don't know, do you, love?"

Kelly frowned, confused. "I don't understand. You know why I suddenly started bawling like a baby?" Disgusted with herself, she started to let her hands drop from where she'd wrapped them around his neck, but he stopped her and put them back where they were.

"You finally let go, love," he told her tenderly. "You finally let go of that reservation, that fear that always reared its ugly head when you felt vulnerable."

Frowning again, she searched his face. "That doesn't make sense." She felt her face turning red. "I've had orgasms, I mean, you've made me come before."

Blade smiled at her but his eyes remained sharp. "Yes, love, but not like you did a little while ago. Before now, you got a sharp rush of pleasure but it never consumed you. Your fear kept you from trusting me enough to really let go. You've been trained to expect pain and fear with intimacy."

"But you spanked me!" Kelly pouted and shivered when his eyes narrowed. "My bottom hurts," she added softly.

"Something tells me that it's only the first of many spankings you're going to earn. Stop squirming on my cock. You're going to get fucked again soon enough."

Kelly looked up at him, enjoying the way his features had tightened. The hand on her bottom shifted the plug inside her.

Kelly gasped and froze.

"Now sit still, so I can finish. I'm retraining your body to associate pain, not pain like someone beating the hell out of you or tearing your insides by raping you, but erotic pain with pleasure. Even while being punished, you had pleasure with the pain."

"Oh." Flustered, Kelly tried to duck her head, but Blade wouldn't let her.

"Yes, oh."

He stood her on her feet and went to deal with the condom, coming back wearing a new one.

Sitting back down, he grasped her hips and lifted her, placing her over his length, and slammed her down onto it. Handling her as though she weighed nothing Blade continued to fuck her hard, sending them both into orbit as he stroked over sensitive tissue that tightened and clenched all around him.

"Come for me, love." Within seconds, Kelly felt her toes curl and her body tighten as she flew into yet another heart stopping climax, not as hard as the last, but somehow more devastating. She watched Blade's face as he came, his features agonized as he went over. God, the image of his face in the throes of passion would forever be branded in her mind.

Afterward he held her, caressing her with soothing hands until they both calmed. She loved this part of being with Blade. Loved the freedom to touch him, she cherished the feel of his strong hands moving over her body tenderly. They wrapped around her, making her feel safe and warm. His desire for her came through and this time with him somehow felt more intimate than the sex.

In the shower, he tickled her as he washed her. "Before long I'll know your body as intimately as my own. We'll see how well you do when I know all your weak spots."

"I think you already know them." Kelly's laugh became a moan when he nibbled at one of those spots.

"Not yet, love." His deep voice rumbled next to her ear, making her shiver yet again. "But I will."

She shifted away to splash water at him. "Wait until I find *your* weak spots and torture you the way you torture me!"

He chuckled, zooming in on another of the spots that drove her wild, making her forget her threats as she became lost in sensation.

They had dried off and started dressing, stopping often when Blade lifted her for a hard kiss or a nuzzle.

"I'm going to go take the plug out," she told him starting for the bathroom door.

"No. The plug stays in. You'll sleep with it inside that tight little ass tonight. You can take it out in the morning."

"But-"

"No, love. It needs to stay in, so I don't hurt you when I take your ass. Do as I say, or else..."

"Maybe I'll find somebody to tie you down and I'll spank you!" She lifted her chin defiantly, hands on her hips.

An evil grin slashed across his face. "Never. I don't sub. Ever. I'm a Dom, love, through and through. And it doesn't just apply to the bedroom."

When he turned to face her fully, the raw power he exuded reminded her once again of his dominance.

"Any woman of mine would have to accept that. It's not a game to me, or just sex. It encompasses everything. I want my woman to be dependant on me for everything and accept that I am in charge and will take care of her. She will obey me and yield to me in all things."

"Jeez, Blade. You don't ask for much, do you?"

"I want it all, Kelly. The woman who shares my life will give herself completely to me and I will cherish and care for her and give her more pleasure than she could ever imagine."

With a last look at Blade, Kelly finished dressing, her heart heavy. She could never be Blade's doll, to pick up and play with or put on a shelf as he wished.

He hadn't spoken of love or feelings for this woman.

Did he already have someone in mind? What if he did? She couldn't imagine life with a man who wanted to own her, his main contribution to the relationship being out of this world orgasms.

Blade drove Kelly home, unsettled by her silence. Had he scared her by talking about permanence, about wanting a woman who looked to him for strength? He purposely hadn't mentioned his feelings for her, not when he knew she didn't want to hear them yet.

Never before had he so desperately wanted to take a woman without a condom. He's never taken a woman bareback, not even in his misspent youth. He never played Russian Roulette that way, he had too much respect for his body and others to do it.

He glanced at her and grimaced. She still frowned, obviously deep in thought as she stared out the windshield. Thinking back to the times he'd teased Jake when Nat drove him crazy, he felt like an idiot. His advice had usually been to spank her and fuck her so hard she forgot all about her anger.

But, he'd slowly come to the realization that being a Dom and being a Dom in love were two different things. As much as he taught Kelly, she taught him.

He frowned thoughtfully. Even his way of teaching Doms in permanent relationships would have to be adjusted.

He needed to get some input from Jake and talk to Royce and King. Blade could see that he'd have to revise some of his teachings, update them to meet the needs of Doms like himself.

There would also be the matter of pregnancy and exploring ways to continue experiencing the Dom/sub lifestyle with children in the house and the obligations that came with it.

His love for Kelly opened his eyes to things he'd never before considered. She'd brought to the surface new challenges, new areas to explore.

Glancing again at his beloved, he worried that he'd pressed too hard. Time to backtrack a little, take her back into her comfort zone before he went away.

Back to sex.

He really hated to leave town now but he had to meet with the rough Dom wannabe before he hurt someone. And, to get a few of his friends to keep an eye on him.

"I'll call you while I'm gone. Don't forget you have an appointment at the spa on Friday."

Delighted with the blush she tried to hide, he added, "I can't wait to put my mouth on that pussy when it's bare."

When she gasped and gaped at him, he chuckled. No matter what, she'll certainly be thinking about him while he's gone.

He grinned to himself.

He'd certainly be thinking of her. He'd lose sleep remembering the sounds she made when she came.

He'd also be thinking about how beautiful she would be, heavy with his child.

Chapter Six

"Blade wouldn't have claimed you, especially in front of that many people if he didn't care about you, Kelly."

"I keep telling you, Jesse, the only reason Blade said that was to keep Clay from spanking me. He wanted to get me out of trouble because he'd already agreed to help me."

Kelly hadn't seen Jesse since Saturday and had spent all day answering her best friend's questions about Blade.

"Blade loves you and you love him." Jesse spun with her hands on her hips. "I can't believe you made that stupid agreement with him!"

Kelly sighed. She'd been watching Jesse pace back and forth in front of the large front window for a half hour now and felt a headache coming on. She resumed restocking the shelves and tried, yet again, to get her friend to understand.

"I told you, Jesse, I wasn't sure if I would be able to let down my guard enough to have sex again. Because of my agreement with Blade, I've discovered that I can."

"Oh, honey, that's wonderful! I told you that you just needed the right man."

Kelly snorted indelicately. "Yeah, right. Up until a couple of months ago, you kept telling me to be careful and not take chances."

She watched, amused, as Jesse turned red.

"I know. I know." She gave Kelly a hug. "It's just that I want you to be as happy as I am. And we got to know Blade. Blade and Simon are as different as night and day."

"I know, Jesse." Kelly shrugged. "But I don't think Blade's in love with me." She held up her hand when Jesse would have interrupted. "I know I love him, but I'm not sure it could work. First, I don't know if I can be what he wants. I don't think I *want* to be what he wants. I used to worry about just being what he needs in the bedroom, or playroom in his case, but after talking to him Saturday night, I'm afraid he wants a puppet."

"A puppet?"

"Yeah," Kelly sighed. "He wants someone who obeys him, does everything he says. He told me he wants a woman who lets him be in charge and will yield to him in all things. I'm not that woman, Jesse. I don't want to be that woman. Simon made me that woman through rapes and beatings and I never want to be that woman again."

Kelly gripped Jesse's arm. "Please try to understand. Don't try to push Blade and I together. I have to work this out in my own way. Because of the agreement I made with Blade, I have six weeks to figure it out."

Jesse regarded her steadily for several long seconds before nodding. "Okay. I won't try to push you and Blade together and I won't say anything to Clay and Rio. But," she added when Kelly would have turned away, "I want you to think about something. There isn't a man in town that doesn't feel the same way as Blade. Clay and Rio gave me the same speech and we fought about it. They always try to get their way."

Flinging her arms heatedly, Jesse continued. "Jake is the same way. If you talk to any of them, they're in charge, their women listen to them, or they'll get a spanking, yada, yada, yada."

Jesse smiled evilly. "Do you see me doing everything Clay and Rio tell me to do? Do I seem like a puppet to you? Does Nat? Yeah, they're tough, they're bossy. But these men care. If Nat's unhappy, Jake would do whatever he could to make her happy again. Clay and Rio are the same. The only time they really put their foot down is when it comes to my health or safety."

Jesse smirked. "You've seen me win against them over and over. You've seen Nat dare Jake to punish her. Do you think she'd do that if she didn't enjoy it? I wonder how many times Jake's been manipulated into turning Nat over his knee."

Kelly couldn't help but grin, knowing Jesse spoke the truth. She sobered. "But Blade and I don't have a relationship. It's just sex and he wants to be in charge."

Jesse shook her head. "These men can say all they want about being in charge, but the bottom line is this. They're only in charge as long as *we* are happy."

Kelly looked up bleakly, her heart heavy. "There's a big difference, Jesse. You and Nat are with men who love you."

Closing up the shop, Kelly carefully avoided Jesse's worried glances. She'd avoided any further conversation about Blade and wanted nothing more than to get upstairs to her apartment, so she didn't have to hear his name any more tonight.

Saying goodnight to Jesse, Frank, and Katy, she made her way upstairs and went straight through her apartment to the tiny bathroom.

Standing in the shower, she let the warm water cascade over her, soothing her and washing away the tears on her face. Knowing she wouldn't be able to go beyond the six weeks with Blade, her movements became slow and lethargic as she got ready for bed.

Wearing a simple cotton gown, Kelly felt cool and comfortable as she settled herself in the oversized chair she'd brought from her apartment in Maryland. Overstuffed and larger than a regular chair, it had become her comfort chair.

Whenever she hurt or felt sad, she curled herself into it with the lightweight, super soft shawl she kept draped over the back. It never failed to soothe her.

She'd used it countless times when Simon hurt her, but since moving to Desire, she'd never needed the soothing effect of the chair until now.

Wrapping the soft shawl around her shoulders, she curled herself into it. Tucking her legs under her, she laid her head on the plush arm and closed her eyes. She really should eat something, but the thought of even fixing herself a sandwich sounded like way too much effort. She couldn't eat anything right now anyway.

The ringing of the phone startled her. She looked down at the display. Seeing Blade's cell phone number, she groaned. She really didn't want to answer, but knew if she didn't, he'd call someone to come check on her. Resigned, she took the call.

"Hello?"

"Hello, love." A pause. "Is something wrong?"

Ignoring the concern in his voice, she closed her eyes again.

"No. I'm just tired. How's your trip going?"

"Not as productive as I would've liked, but I've done all I can do for now. I'll be home tomorrow. Why are you so tired?"

"No reason. Just tired. Have a safe trip home tomorrow."

"Kelly?"

Kelly's eyes snapped open at the sharp tone.

"Yes?" She pulled the shawl tighter around her.

"Are you sure you're all right?"

"I'm fine, Blade, just tired. I was almost asleep when you called. Can we talk another time?"

"Of course, love. Sleep well. I'll see you tomorrow."

"Goodnight." Kelly hung up before he could say anything else. She just wanted to escape in sleep for a while.

After a good night's sleep, she'd be better equipped to face Blade again.

Blade stared at his cell phone frowning. Kelly hadn't sounded like herself at all. He hated being away from her, especially this early in their relationship. Unsettled now, he couldn't shake the feeling that she would do her best to talk herself out of their agreement if he didn't get back to Desire soon.

She'd been fine the other night until he'd mentioned a permanent relationship. After that she'd been quiet and morose.

Rubbing a hand over his face in frustration, he went to the mini bar and poured himself a drink. Staring out the window, he watched the storm rage angrily in the night sky and wanted to be home.

He'd thought for sure that Kelly loved him and responded so well to him because of it. But, in that case, she would have shown a little more enthusiasm when he'd hinted at having a relationship instead of the damned agreement they'd made.

Why hadn't he said no to it?

Hindsight was definitely twenty-twenty.

He feared she'd become so bottled up sexually that she would have the same kind of reaction to anyone who took time with her.

A sudden thought occurred to him and he ruthlessly pushed it aside. *No fucking way!* As much as he tried to dismiss it, the idea kept coming back. It could backfire on him in a big way. But wouldn't it be better to know the truth? Pouring himself another drink, he grimaced when he saw that his hand shook.

"Fuck."

He put the glass down before he gave in to the urge to throw it. Resigned, he pulled out his cell phone and punched in a series of numbers.

Clenching the phone tightly, he closed his eyes in agony as he waited.

"Royce."

Blade took a deep breath and forced the words out. "Royce, I need a favor."

Kelly glanced up when Jesse came into the back room with Rachel in tow.

Boone and Chase had just finished with the new cabinets and kitchen area. As they cleared the mess, they made several trips in and out as they put their tools back in their truck. Walking back in, they looked up and froze when they saw Rachel.

Uh oh, Jesse the matchmaker strikes again. Kelly knew Jesse felt the undercurrents, the tension that suddenly made it difficult to breathe, but she continued as though she noticed nothing.

"Rachel, you have to see what a great job Boone and Chase did with the back room." Jesse smiled warmly at the men as she started to show Rachel the changes that had been made. "Remember how it used to be? It was just a kitchen for the house with those old kitchen cabinets that we could never get organized. Not enough space and no way to divide our scents."

Kelly hid a smile as Jesse went on and on. She blithely ignored the tension and the looks that passed between the two men and Rachel as they tried to ignore each other. The entire time the men and Rachel snuck glances at each other.

"Look at all the new organized space we have, along with a little kitchen area for us to use. Aren't Boone and Chase incredible?"

"Incredible," Rachel muttered.

When both men glared at her, Rachel turned away, blinking rapidly.

Boone looked devastated and Chase stepped forward, but Rachel wouldn't look at them. She followed Jesse, who tried to convince her of the benefits of adding such organized space to her store.

Still avoiding the men's eyes, Rachel jumped when her cell phone rang.
"Hello? Oh, hi Blade."

Boone and Chase's faces fell, as they stared at Rachel. Kelly's stomach clenched, feeling the same jealousy that showed clearly on their faces.

"Yes, of course. I did everything you asked," Rachel laughed playfully. "Yes, they are. So, I'll see you this afternoon? Great! I'll see you then."

Putting the phone away, Rachel looked at Boone and Chase. "So would you be able to do something like this at my place?"

"Sure," Chase muttered while Boone simply stood glaring at her.

"Great. When you come over, I'll show you my bras and panties."

Chase looked stunned while Boone's face hardened even more.

"Excuse me?" Boone asked tightly.

"Well aren't you going to need to see the things I want organized before you decide what I'll need?" Rachel asked, all innocence.

"Uh, yeah." Chase cleared his throat.

Rachel appeared to have a hard time hiding a smile. "You'll need to see how many different styles I have, too. There are the regular panties, French cut, thongs, oh, and the crotchless panties, not to mention the edible ones."

"We'll get back to you," Boone growled and walked out, slamming the door behind him.

"What did Blade want?" Chase demanded.

Kelly looked at Rachel, wanting to know the same thing.

Rachel's eyes narrowed. "What do you care?"

"What. Did. Blade. Want?"

Chase looked like he desperately wanted to close in on Rachel and shake her. Jesse took a step toward Rachel, but Rachel shook her head and faced Chase head on.

"It's really none of your business."

Chase stepped forward and leaned down, his face just inches from Rachel's "I can make it my business."

Kelly blinked. She'd never heard that tone from the flirtatious Chase before. Worried, she glanced at Jesse, who hid a grin.

Oh, Lord.

Rachel didn't even flinch. She met Chase's eyes squarely. "Go for it cowboy."

Several seconds passed as Chase struggled for control. Kelly recognized the look, having seen it on Blade's face often enough.

Finally, Chase smiled the kind of smile that sent a shiver through anyone who saw it. "This isn't over, doll." Running a finger down Rachel's cheek, he murmured, "We'll see you soon."

The back door slammed as Chase stormed out.

Rachel slumped, blowing out a breath, and grasping the counter for support. "Whew. That was fun," she murmured dryly.

"Are you okay?" Kelly asked, concerned. Rachel moved to the window, wincing as the men sprayed gravel as they peeled out of the parking lot. Seeing Rachel's interest in Boone and Chase, Kelly couldn't resist asking. "Is there anything between you and Blade?"

Rachel winced. "Sorry about that. I just wanted to see if I could get a rise out of those two knuckleheads. Apparently it worked, huh?"

Jesse helped Rachel to a chair. "Yeah, well maybe you'd better not do that again."

"You think?" Rachel accepted the bottle of water Jesse handed her with a smile.

Reaching out to lay a hand on Kelly's arm, Rachel smiled reassuringly. "The only thing between Blade and me is business, which you'll find out soon enough. It's supposed to be a secret, but he's been ordering stuff for you for weeks. Please don't let on that I told you. I just don't want you to think there's something between us. There isn't."

Kelly smiled. "I think Blade tried to make them jealous the other day. He kept talking to them about your panties."

Rachel grinned. "I know. He told me. That's why, when he called just now, I took it as an opportunity to see if I could get a reaction out of those two. Blade suspected something was wrong by the way I sounded and asked if they were close."

"Well, you got a reaction all right." Jesse patted Rachel on the shoulder. "I thought Chase would grab you, throw you over his shoulder and storm out."

Rachel laughed. "Not every man is like Clay or Rio."

"Yeah, I know." Jesse smirked. "But what is going on with the three of you? It's obvious you're crazy about them and they're definitely nuts about you." Jesse frowned. "What's the problem?"

"I have no idea," Rachel sighed. "Ever since I moved here two years ago, I've seen them watch me. They wouldn't even talk to me for the longest time. Chase is such a flirt. You've seen him in action. He flirts with every woman in town. Except me."

Jesse sipped her own water. "I heard that they did really well building high dollar houses and condos, shopping centers, all kinds of stuff. They made a fortune. Then for some reason, they sold their company and moved back here. They have more than enough money, but they do work like this," Jesse gestured toward the new cabinets, "to stay busy."

Rachel's eyes widened incredulously. "Where do you hear all this stuff?"

Jesse smirked. "Nat. She told me that when Boone and Chase came back to town, they stayed drunk for a month. She thinks it had something to do with a woman."

Kelly watched Rachel pale and felt sorry for her. "You don't think they're in love with someone else, do you?"

"Nope," Jesse answered confidently. "Not and look at you like they do. But, I think someone has hurt them and they're scared to go after you."

"Great," Rachel muttered.

Kelly knew Jesse well enough to be wary of the glint in her eye.

"We'll just have to make them get over their fear." Jesse smiled mischievously, standing when she heard a customer come in. "We'll have to find out just what it would take to push them over the edge." She turned and headed out toward the front.

Rachel grimaced as she looked over at Kelly. "She's a lot like Nat, isn't she?"

Kelly couldn't prevent a smile. "You have no idea. They're both very protective of their friends and champion matchmakers. They've decided that everyone should be as happy as they are."

Rachel nervously played with the bottle of water in front of her. "Well if Jesse tries to get Boone, Chase, and I together, she's doomed to fail."

Kelly laughed. The relief of knowing there was nothing going on between Rachel and Blade made her giddy. "Oh, ye of little faith. Jesse will just have to step up her game. If that doesn't work, she'll pull in the big guns and get Nat involved. Boone and Chase will never know what hit them!"

After Rachel left, Kelly busied herself by putting the last of the supplies away in the new storage units. She now had plenty of space for the new scents she wanted to order.

She'd finished the first scent for the men's line they wanted to create. It had taken quite a while to get the citrus based scent just right. Now she had to start on the men's products and find time to work on another scent for the men. Maybe something with musk.

The bottles for the men's shampoo Jesse had ordered had finally arrived and Kelly wanted to get started.

When she heard the back door open, she didn't turn from where she labeled shelves. "I think those two boxes are the last ones, Frank. Boone and Chase do fantastic work, don't they?"

When he didn't answer, Kelly turned with a smile.

And froze.

Blade stood, leaning against the counter. Wearing faded jeans and a black t shirt that lovingly hugged his chest and biceps. He looked rough and masculine and good enough to eat.

With his hair tied back, her attention focused on his eyes. Her breath caught at the glittering hunger in them.

"Hi, Blade." Kelly struggled to contain her response to him. Jeez, one look and her nipples already demanded his attention.

"Hi, Blade," he mimicked. "Is that all you have to say to me? Get over here and give me my kiss."

Kelly raised her eyes coyly even as her pussy clenched at his tone. "What kiss?"

"My 'welcome home, I missed you, Blade' kiss, you little minx. Come here."

Kelly obediently moved to Blade, lifting her face eagerly. She saw the heat in his eyes before hers fluttered closed as his lips touched hers.

Man, he could kiss.

She felt her knees weaken when his tongue pushed deep, stroking hers possessively. When he lifted his head, she moaned. The taste of him never failed to intoxicate her.

His fingers traced her moist lips and she involuntarily touched her tongue to them. "I missed you, love. Did you wear the plug all night Saturday like I told you?"

"Hmm, mmm," Kelly nodded weakly.

Blade chuckled. "Go tell Jesse you'll be back in a few minutes. I need to put the next plug in your ass."

A jolt of lust went through her. "Now?"

"Now." He fingered her choker. "I see the cabinets are done. Did Chase flirt with you?"

Kelly rolled her eyes. "Chase flirts with everybody except... I'll go tell Jesse."

Blade grabbed her arm when she would have moved away. "Everyone except...Rachel?"

Kelly shrugged, not wanting to betray any confidences.

"You're not still jealous of Rachel, are you?" Blade asked frowning.

Kelly shrugged again. "She's beautiful and you seemed interested in her. I know it's none of my business."

Blade touched a finger to her lips, silencing her. "Rachel is very beautiful, but she's not a pint sized firecracker who responds so beautifully. The only woman I'm interested in is you. Go tell Jesse you'll be back in half an hour." He turned her and swatted her bottom to get her moving.

Upstairs in her apartment, Kelly shook with arousal as Blade undid her jeans and pulled both them and her panties down to her knees.

"Where's the other plug?"

When Kelly pointed to her nightstand, Blade opened the drawer and took the plug out of it. He pulled a larger plug out of a bag she hadn't noticed before, along with a brand new tube of lube. He dropped the smaller plug in the bag and tossed it aside.

"I'll leave the lube here since we'll need it again."

The promise in his eyes made her senses spiral. She felt so vulnerable and naughty standing with her back to him and her bottom exposed while he remained fully dressed.

"Bend over, love." Even when using an endearment, she couldn't mistake the steel in his command. "Knees on the bed. Good girl. No, not on your hands. Put your shoulders on the bed. Stick that ass way up for me. Good girl."

Kelly's slit dripped as she felt Blade work the cool lube into her bottom.

"Ohh." She fisted her hands in the bedcovers. Pressing her face into them, she struggled to stifle her moans when she felt the plug start to push into her. Blade used the shallow strokes he'd used before, fucking her ass with the plug, each stroke deeper than the last.

She couldn't keep from pushing back onto the plug. Her bottom opened to him, already succumbing to his desires. She needed the erotic pain and pleasure only he could give her.

"That's it, love. Your ass loves to be fucked. Wait until I get my cock inside you. You're so tight. When I open your ass with my cock, you're going to squeeze me so tight it's going to be agony."

His words drew erotic images in her head that sent her higher even as he reached around and began to stroke her clit.

"I can't wait," he growled.

The last of the plug pushed inside her just as her orgasm began.

"It's too big," were the only words she could get out before she went up in flames, consumed by wildfire. It went on and on as Blade slowed the strokes on her clit, dragging it out until Kelly could no longer stand it.

"Please, no more!" She begged, but then felt his cock at her drenched entrance.

"Yes, love, more!" With that, he thrust into her to the hilt.

Bent over like this, she felt Blade go deeper than ever and had no way of controlling his thrusts. With the jeans keeping her legs immobile and his hand pressing her shoulders to the bed, she lay immobile, helpless to do anything.

She loved it!

His thrusts became deep and deliberate. Without warning, she came again, muffling her scream in the bedcovers. Her pussy clenched on him repeatedly as his thrusts came faster. It intensified the full feeling in her bottom and made it burn. But she couldn't seem to stop. She heard Blade's growl as he held himself deep and knew she'd taken him with her.

Blade covered her body with his own, surrounding her with his heat and strength as they both breathed heavily. After several long minutes, he lifted himself off of her and helped her to stand. Between nips and feather light kisses, he straightened her clothing, pulling her jeans and panties up over where the plug filled her.

"I want this plug to stay right where it is until tomorrow morning. Do you hear me?"

"Yes, Blade," Kelly answered, still weak from her orgasm.

"Good girl." He turned her in his arms and pulled her close, cupping her head against his shoulder as he stroked her back. "I have some things to do tonight. I'll see you tomorrow. Now give me my kiss."

Kelly smiled, snuggling against his chest. "What kiss?"

"The 'goodbye' kiss, the 'I love the plug in my bottom, but I don't want to skip the rest before you fuck my ass' kiss."

"Oh."

"Yeah, oh."

Kelly lifted her face obediently, ignoring Blade's chuckled, "I thought that would get you."

"You always know how to get me," Kelly breathed before his lips touched hers.

This kiss had a different flavor. His lips touched hers lightly, searching, coaxing as he nibbled gently. She wondered absently just how many ways of kissing Blade had mastered.

Not being able to stand it any longer, she pulled his head down, wrapping her arms tightly around his neck as she pushed her tongue greedily past his lips, hungry for his taste.

He obliged her, deepening the kiss, cupping her bottom and lifting her, pulling her thighs up until they wrapped around his waist. When he lifted his head, hers dropped weakly to his shoulder. Strong fingers pressed on the base of the plug, forcing a moan from her. "Demanding little minx, aren't you?"

Kelly pouted, her eyes full of mischief. "I only wanted a kiss."

"Well, you got one. Now, you have to get back to work and I have to get back to the club. Leave the plug in."

Kelly nodded and he lowered her to her feet.

They left her apartment and she walked back down to the shop with him and into the back room.

She started when Blade slapped her bottom sharply.

"Keep your hands and fingers away from your pussy and clit tonight. No coming without permission, remember?"

When his hands cupped her breasts, Kelly shuddered. "I remember."

"Good girl." He caressed her bottom, making her tremble. "I'll see you tomorrow."

Chapter Seven

Slipping her shoes on the next morning, Kelly jolted when her cell phone rang. Seeing Blade's number on the display, she took a deep breath. She'd been aroused since he left yesterday and had come up to her apartment after work with every intention of giving herself the release she needed. But every time she'd tried, she'd pictured Blade's face and cool command and her efforts became futile. Damn him! Still angry and aroused, she answered.

"Hello?"

"Good morning, love."

"Good morning, Blade. How are you?"

"Good. And you?"

"I'm fine, thanks. I'm just getting ready to go downstairs."

"So early? I thought I'd catch you still under the covers. I imagined you warm and sleep soft, your hair mussed, and the plug I pushed into you still in your bottom."

Kelly closed her eyes imagining Blade joining her in the picture he'd painted in her head. Shaking it off, she kept her voice cool.

"No, I'm going in early. I have a lot of work to do. We're starting on the new men's line."

"I can't wait to try it. Is something wrong?"

"No. I just need to get to work. My work is as important to me as your work is to you."

"Did I say it wasn't?"

Kelly felt a cold shiver down her spine at Blade's tone.

"No, but I thought you should be reminded. I may have to work on Saturday."

"No. You won't."

"But-"

"In case you've forgotten, you've already promised the weekend to me. Are you backing out?"

"No, but-"

"Good. I'll be by after work to insert your new plug. It would be sooner, but I have a few appointments today."

"Doms and their subs?" Kelly tried to keep the insecurity from her voice.

"Among other things. Royce, King, and I have a variety of business interests and yes, Doms and their subs are a big part of that business."

"Are you going to be touching these women?" Kelly cursed herself for blurting out her thoughts.

"Probably. If not this time, then another. You know what I do, Kelly. What's all this about?"

"Nothing, Blade. Look, you do what you have to do and so will I. I'd better get to work."

"Be careful, love. You're pissing me off."

"Sorry." Kelly muttered, sounding anything but. Jealousy and arousal made her bitchy. Oh, hell. She couldn't let it get to her like this. He'd be out of her life in a few short weeks and she wanted to enjoy the time she had left with him.

"You're perilously close to having your bottom reddened after I push the next plug into you."

"I'm so sorry, Blade," she couldn't help replying sarcastically.

Blade muttered something under his breath.

"What?"

"Never mind," he replied in a soft voice. "I'll see you after work."

Kelly frowned at the phone after he'd disconnected. Blade had sounded really strange. She'd expected anger at her bitchiness. Something inside her needed to push him. But his soft voice at the end of the conversation worried her.

She felt the change in herself since first being with him. Her confidence had grown and she knew Blade had caused it. She liked it and she didn't want to go back to feeling like a scared little girl ever again. Perhaps Blade didn't care for her newfound self-esteem. If he wanted her to remain timid, he would be greatly disappointed. She couldn't stay that way even for him. She needed him to want the person that emerged from the shell she'd protected herself with all this time.

But, she wouldn't give up this time with him. She deserved it and maybe Blade would start to like her newfound confidence.

Kelly went down the stairs and into the former kitchen. Pulling out the items she needed, she forced herself to stop thinking about Blade. Thinking about the inevitable end to their relationship only depressed her.

After showering, she rifled through her closet, looking for something sexy to wear. When she heard a knock on her door, she laid aside the pink sundress she'd chosen and went to answer it. Knowing it would be Blade, she took a calming breath.

Opening the door, all the breath left her body. Blade, dressed in a well faded pair of jeans and a white t-shirt stood leaning against the door jam. His jeans hugged his thighs lovingly and the t-shirt showed off his chest to perfection.

His black hair hung loose and shiny, and Kelly wanted nothing more than to grab handfuls of it and pull him down to attack those sinful lips.

"Hello, Blade." That didn't come out as cool as she meant it to. Turning away from temptation, Kelly moved into the small living room. "I was just about to call you. We'll have to do this another time. Jesse invited me to eat with them tonight. Clay and Rio are barbequing.

"Yes, I know. Rio called to invite me this afternoon."

She started when hands on her shoulders turned her to face him. She hadn't even heard him move. When he cupped the back of her head and started to lower his lips to hers, she could no longer fight the temptation.

Grabbing handfuls of his hair, she smashed her lips into his and levered herself up to wrap her legs around his waist. Naked beneath her robe, she felt it part and gasped at the heat when her body touched his.

His hot hands gripped her bottom. She pressed her breasts against his soft cotton shirt, the heat of his body blazing through and setting her nipples on fire. Wriggling in his embrace, she winced when her folds scraped over his belt buckle.

"Easy, love. No more of that." Adjusting her position, he walked to the sofa and laid her carefully on the cushions. "Let me kiss it and make it better."

"Blade, no. I…" When Blade's tongue swept her folds, she forgot everything else. His hands held her thighs high and wide as his mouth became more and more demanding. Within seconds, she raced toward an orgasm.

He knew exactly how to completely unravel her so quickly she couldn't catch her breath, much less fight what he made her feel.

Knowing that he did this on purpose, to claim dominance over her, she fought the impending orgasm with everything she had. She needed to challenge him.

He kept her poised on the razor sharp edge, showing her with every stroke of his tongue that he could push her over at any time.

And still she fought it.

Finally, being unable to stand it anymore, she stopped fighting. She'd become too far gone she no longer cared about showing Blade anything, didn't care that he would punish her for coming without permission, didn't care if her apartment came falling down around her. Whimpering in frustration, she admitted defeat.

His mouth continued to ravage her throbbing clit. Her pussy wept and clenched, the emptiness unbearable.

She couldn't come.

Whimpering, and then sobbing with need and frustration, her body shaking uncontrollably, Kelly whipped her head from side to side in agony. She couldn't bear it.

"Come for me."

The word no sooner left Blade's mouth then a fireball exploded deep inside her body, burning her with its heat. Every nerve ending burst with pleasure as sensation on top of sensation ripped through her. Her body jerked out of control as though being touched by a live wire. When the jerking finally stopped, her body shimmered and tingled and she wouldn't have been at all surprised to see that she glowed.

She didn't know how much time had passed before she became aware of Blade's soft crooning or the soothing strokes on her back as he held her against his chest, her head lying heavily on his shoulder.

Several long minutes later, Kelly finally had the energy to lift her head. "I didn't come until you said to."

Blade chuckled and kissed her. "No, love, you didn't."

Kelly frowned. "I wanted to. I tried to."

Blade's lips curled. "Did you?"

"Yeah, but I couldn't." She shrugged. "We'd better hurry or we'll be late. Don't you want to...?"

"I'm not interested in a quickie right now. I didn't particularly care for your tone this morning on the phone. I also don't care for your jealousy. Even though right now we only have an agreement, I've told you that during the time I'm training you, I will not be fucking another woman. The only women that I touch will be in the presence of their master, and business only."

His icy gaze froze her in place. She couldn't look away, even though she desperately wanted to.

"I don't care for the fact that you don't trust me. I mean what I say, Kelly. Always."

Kelly extricated herself from his arms and stood, perfectly aware that she could only because he'd allowed it. Striding several feet away, she turned to see him sprawled on her sofa, one ankle crossed over the opposite knee. Except for the cold look in his eyes and the obvious bulge in his jeans, he looked totally relaxed.

Determined to keep her eyes off the bulge, she looked into his eyes.

"How would you feel if a man came in and wanted me to massage his cock with massage oil, so he could see how well the product worked?" She shrugged. "After all, it would be business, nothing personal."

"I would kill him and beat your ass raw," Blade told her negligently as though discussing the weather. "My business is about pleasure between consenting adults. It's also about safety, teaching men how to inflict erotic pain in a safe manner, so their subs are not injured in a way that is extreme or from which they can't recover. I've seen it far too often."

Blade rose deliberately and strode over to her, grabbing her shoulders, all semblance of relaxed male gone.

"Do you have any idea how many men do to their subs what Simon did to you, telling themselves it's okay because they're Doms? What I do is a helluva lot different from some horny asshole wanting his dick massaged by a beautiful woman."

Kelly stood in stunned silence, not knowing what to say as Blade continued.

"What Royce, King, and I do is important, Kelly. Yes, sometimes it's just pointers on how to bring their subs the most pleasure, where and how to touch, delaying or preventing an orgasm, but a lot is about safety. That's our main priority and I won't stop, not for you or anyone else. You're going to have to learn to accept that."

Shocked and moved by how strongly he and the others felt about protecting the women who trusted enough to be subs, Kelly blushed, ashamed at herself for thinking the men did this just for fun and games.

Knowing how protective he and the others had been, none of this should have surprised her. It humbled her to realize how much they considered a woman's safety and had made it their main priority.

Her jealousy had blinded her to his motives. She still didn't like that he touched other women, but now understood him much better.

"I understand, Blade. I'm glad you're the way you are. It's something for me to think about." She couldn't really say more without giving herself away. They only had an agreement after all.

She looked up at him warily. "So it's okay if we don't do this tonight?"

"Oh, you're going to have that ass filled, but not now. I'd rather Clay and Rio didn't know you have a plug in your ass at dinner. Besides, because of your attitude this morning, my hand's going to heat up that ass before I put the plug in. I'd rather you be able to sit for dinner. Now, get dressed, so we can go. I'm starving."

Kelly unconsciously clenched the cheeks of her bottom at Blade's threat. "How would they know? Do you tell them what you do to me?" she asked in horror.

Did everyone know what went on in Blade's playroom?

"Of course not," he snapped impatiently. "What happens between us is private. But," he added with a grin, "Clay and Rio can spot a woman with a plug in her ass three blocks away."

"People can tell?" Kelly asked, intrigued.

Blade laughed. "Not everyone, love. I'd say that most of the men in Desire can, though."

He leaned down to whisper conspiratorially in her ear, "It's the way they walk."

"The way they…? Forget it. I have to get dressed."

She ignored Blade's chuckle as she reached for her clothes.

Kelly always had a good time at the Erickson's. They demonstrated the love they all felt for each other in hundreds of ways, filling the house with laughter and happiness. Through it all, the boy's antics kept them all entertained.

Clay's son, Will, Rio's son, Kyle, and Jesse's son, Alex, shared the house next door, the one Clay and Rio had lived in before building the one they and Jesse lived in now. They'd built it with Boone and Chase's help while waiting for their perfect woman. They'd moved into it with Jesse as soon as they'd tricked her into picking out the furniture for it.

The boys currently spent their time fixing up the old house and lived there while they did the renovations before they started their next college semester. Clay and Rio got a kick out of helping the boys, but didn't take over.

Boone and Chase also helped out when they needed it, but everyone wanted the boys to do it together, so they would consider it their home.

Kelly couldn't help but smile when she saw her best friend's glow. Jesse never stopped smiling as she listened to her husbands and the three boys. All through dinner, the boys talked excitedly about today's progress.

"You should have seen it, Jesse. Dad thought the water was off, so he loosened the pipe under the kitchen sink." Kyle laughed so hard they could barely understand him.

Will and Alex laughed just as hard while Clay chuckled. Rio tried hard to look stern, but his eyes gleamed with mirth.

"You should have seen Uncle Rio when the water hit him in the face," Will added, laughing so hard Kelly thought he would fall off the chair. "He couldn't get it turned off."

"Mom, you should have been there." Alex wiped his eyes. "Clay heard all the yelling and ran in and slid on his butt on the wet floor, and ran straight into Rio. It was so funny, like in a movie."

Everyone laughed so hard that they'd stopped eating. The adults recovered first as the boys continued to laugh hysterically.

Jesse still smiled as she looked at the boys affectionately. "And what were you three angels doing while all of this was going on?"

This sent the boys into fresh peals of laughter.

Clay chuckled and shook his head at the boys before smiling at his wife ruefully. "Pretty much what they're doing now."

Still laughing, they heard a knock at the door, and a smiling Rio got up to answer it.

Several minutes later he returned, no longer smiling. The jovial mood at the table vanished abruptly when the sheriff followed Rio into the room, his face grim.

Kelly's eyes automatically flew to Jesse to find her friend staring back at her, her face deathly white.

Clay cursed as he pulled Jesse onto his lap and wrapped his arms around her. Blade pulled Kelly close, wrapping his arm protectively around her shoulder.

"Have a seat, Ace. Hungry?" Rio gestured to the chair he'd vacated and leaned against the counter.

"No, thanks." Ace grimaced. "I'm sorry to interrupt your dinner, but I have some news for all of you." He looked at Blade. "King told me you were here, and I thought it would be better to talk to all of you together."

Rio placed a cup of coffee in front of the sheriff and sat in Jesse's chair, reaching for her hand. The boys' eyes looked huge in their faces as they watched the adults, their dinner forgotten.

"Everything's okay, guys. It's nothing we can't handle," Rio told them reassuringly.

"What is it, Ace?" Clay asked softly.

The sheriff leaned forward, looking over at Jesse's son, Alex and smiling apologetically. "Ever since Jesse's ex husband, Brian, went to jail for beating the hell out of her, I've kept tabs on him. I've also kept trying to locate Simon."

He glanced at Kelly. "If your ex boyfriend plans to come to Desire, I want to know about it."

Kelly felt the rest of the blood drain from her face as she looked over at Jesse, who didn't look any better.

Ace looked up. "Simon visited Brian."

Kelly gasped and gripped Blade's hand as the sheriff continued.

"The guard said that evidently Brian got Simon all worked up, telling him about their women moving away and 'Who the hell did they think they were, trying to get away from them'? The guard said they both got so upset, he had to settle them down."

"Damn it!" Clay growled, tightening his hold on Jesse as though Simon would come through the door at any minute and rip her from his arms. She felt Blade's hold tighten on her and felt the men's eyes on her.

"Yeah," Ace nodded. "According to the guard I spoke to, Brian had Simon in a rage. I have to assume he's on his way here."

Kelly trembled as she looked over at Jesse. "I'm not going to hide from him," she told Jesse defiantly, anticipating her.

"But Kelly—," Jesse began.

"No, Jesse. I'm not the same person I used to be." She glanced at Blade, seeing the anger and fear he made no attempt to hide.

"If you think you're going to take this guy on, you'd better think again!"

Kelly pulled away from Blade, stood, and began to pace the kitchen. "I'm not stupid. I'm not going after him. He's bigger and stronger than I am. But, I'm not going to hide from him either. I want this to be over."

She spun to face Jesse. "How long have I lived in fear because of Simon? I'm tired of it. I'm pissed off because I've allowed it. No more, Jesse."

Kelly wiped a hand over her face, surprised to find it wet with tears, but when Jesse stood and crossed to her, she met her squarely. "Didn't we come here to start over?"

"Yes, we did. And we did start over. But I think you should move in with us until Simon is caught."

"Absolutely." Rio stood and moved closer, running his hand down her arm. "And someone will be at the store every day."

"No," Kelly shook her head. Rio moved aside as Blade stood and approached her.

Blade wrapped an arm around her waist, pulling her close. "You'll stay at the club with me," Blade told her, his voice like cold steel.

"For how long?" she asked and shook her head. "No. Simon could wait days or even weeks to show up if he shows up at all."

She pulled away from Blade and walked to the French doors looking out at the horses in the distance. "I'm not letting Simon upset my life ever again. If he does show up, he'll see I'm not the same scared little girl he beat up on!"

She looked at the sheriff. "How long ago did Simon go to see Brian?"

Ace stood and walked over to refill his cup, watching her. "Ten days ago. And I'm wondering if Brian talked him into coming for both of you."

"Christ," Clay muttered, wiping a hand over his face.

"Yeah, and I knew nothing until today. Believe me, the guard got an earful." He looked at each of the men in turn. "My deputies will pass pictures of Simon all over town. Everyone will watch for him. Here's a few for you to show your men."

When Blade took one, Kelly averted her eyes. She never wanted to see the face in that picture again.

Ace looked at the boys. "If any of you see this man, you stay away from him. Call me."

The boys nodded enthusiastically, caught up in the drama.

"I don't want anyone else hurt!" Kelly moved back to the table and faced the others.

"I don't want *you* hurt, damn it!" Blade sat back down next to her and grabbed her arm. "You will never be alone until he's caught and I really don't give a damn if you like it or not. The bastard is *not* going to get the chance to hurt you again!"

"I hate that you're all involved in this," Kelly groaned.

"Too bad," Blade muttered unapologetically. "We'll have to show Frank the pictures and one of us should be at the shop at all times." He gestured to the three boys. "There's room at the club if you want them away from here."

For the first time since Ace walked in, the men laughed as they looked at the hopeful expressions on the boys faces.

"We'd never get them to come home again," Clay told him, smiling at the boys.

"I want them here."

Jesse's low monotone grabbed everyone's attention. Clay and Rio watched her worriedly as she continued.

"He'll watch her to see if she goes anywhere alone. She won't. He'll watch the store and try to get to her that way if he sees a chance."

She rubbed her arms as if she was cold and she regarded her husbands steadily. "I want the boys here. If Simon can't get to Kelly, he might find me here. He knows I'll know where she is. He's unstable and Brian may have told him to bring Alex back with him." She sighed and rubbed her forehead. "There's a security system here and the boys could find their way around all the out buildings in the dark. There are plenty of places that they could hide. Simon could never corner them here."

Kelly sighed in relief when the men agreed with Jesse. At least she wouldn't be disrupting the boys' lives.

The men talked, making plans. She tuned them out and looked over at her best friend. "We sure did bring a lot of trouble with us, didn't we, Jesse?"

Silence filled the room as Jesse nodded sadly and moved to stare out the window.

Ace, who had just raised his coffee mug to his lips, froze and lowered it back to the table. "If the two of you are blaming yourselves for the actions of these men, you're going to piss me off."

"You're going to piss all of us off," Blade eyed them both hotly.

Kelly glanced up at Blade in surprise, startled to see his control shaken.

Kelly looked over at Alex, feeling sorry for him. With a hand on Alex's shoulders, Rio smiled reassuringly at his stepson. Poor thing. Kelly knew he would feel guilty about his father's part in all of this.

Clay leaned back in his chair and folded his arms over his chest, adopting 'the look' as Jesse called it. "No one is going to get the chance to get to either one of you. We protect what's ours."

He shook his head grimly. "You all are part of this town now, and no one is going to be able to hurt you here." He muttered under his breath. "Unless one of us screws up."

"But my apartment has an alarm." Kelly gestured toward Clay and Rio. "They had it installed and it's a good one. Why can't I just stay there? Jesse did when Brian was…" Kelly clamped her mouth shut, but it was too late. She knew she'd lost this argument.

"Yeah," Ace muttered grimly. "And before we could stop him, he'd already beaten you both so badly, you had to be taken to the hospital."

Blade gripped her chin and turned her to face him. "That is *not* going to happen again!"

When Alex ran out of the room, Jesse followed.

"Christ, I'm sorry," Ace muttered in disgust.

Clay stood to follow his wife. "We'll take care of it. Believe me, Alex knows we're all trying to protect the women. He understands."

"I feel so bad," Kelly sighed. "All of this trouble because we moved here."

Blade pulled her close. "The difference is this time you have a whole town behind you."

Chapter Eight

Kelly woke Friday morning, smiling when she felt Blade's lips on her forehead.

"Time to wake up, sleepyhead. I'll go get us some breakfast from the diner and meet you downstairs. Clay and Rio should be here by now. Then we'll talk to Frank."

Kelly opened her eyes to see that Blade had already showered and dressed, his hair still damp. He looked so damned gorgeous. She still couldn't believe that, for now at least, he belonged to her. Sometimes her mouth went dry just looking at him.

She wished he'd woken her earlier so she could have showered with him. When they'd showered together before, it had been intimate and playful. Perhaps he'd decided that it had been *too* intimate for the kind of relationship they had.

Brushing the depressing thought from her mind, she promised herself that she wouldn't let it ruin her mood. She would try her best this opportunity to be with Blade one day at a time.

She stretched languorously, her body deliciously sore. Blade had wrung several orgasms from her during the night in his attempt to take her mind off of Simon. He'd held her in his arms as they dozed, only to waken her by slowly, thoroughly arousing her again.

As much as she loved the mind numbing orgasms, the quieter times became much more precious to her. Being held securely in Blade's arms, his hands caressing her soothingly as shudders continued to run through her, made her feel special and cared for.

The deep demanding kisses before and during became gentle and possessive afterward. As they dozed, he'd held her firmly spooned against him, his arms heavy bands closed around her, effectively shutting out the rest of the world. Cocooned in warmth and intimacy, she felt cherished, something she'd never felt before.

"Blade," she breathed as he sat on the bed next to her.

Every time he'd taken her, he'd insisted that she say his name over and over. So, she had, until the end, when she'd screamed it.

"Hmmm? What is it, love?"

If only she could tell him the way she felt about him. She wanted to, more than anything, but with nothing settled between them, it would have to wait. Struggling for something to say, she suddenly remembered.

"Today's spa day."

"That it is." He answered, frowning slightly.

"What's wrong?"

"Nothing, love. I just wonder how long you think you're going to get away with lying to me. Hurry up and get ready. I'm hungry."

He picked up the two bags she'd packed the night before. Without looking at her, he walked toward the door. "I'll put these in the truck and take them with me to the club later."

Kelly frowned as she watched him go, disturbed by his abrupt mood change.

Last night when they got back from Jesse's he'd made her pack several days worth of clothing to take to the club with her. Afterward, he'd kept her too occupied to think about Simon. Just now, he'd been annoyed with her and she didn't know what she could do about it. It's not like she could tell him the truth. She wanted this time with him and didn't want to think about Simon.

Why couldn't Simon just leave her the hell alone?

It's not like he loved her. They'd never married or even talked about it. But he'd always been adamant that she would never get away from him.

Throwing off depressing thoughts of Simon, Kelly showered, dressed quickly, and went downstairs to find everyone drinking coffee and waiting for her. When Blade saw her, he poured her a cup, and gestured that she sit.

"You need to eat something. You hardly touched your dinner last night."

When Frank arrived, the men showed him the picture of Simon, explaining the circumstances as Kelly and Jesse cleared the remnants of breakfast and opened the shop.

"What about the girls?" Kelly asked worriedly, suddenly remembering. "I'd never forgive myself if Simon hurt one of them."

"They're taking a paid vacation," Jesse replied. "The men are going to be here anyway," she added before Kelly could say anything. Jesse grinned at her. "If we get busy, they can help us out. I kind of like the idea of being able to boss them around for a change."

"For a change?" Clay asked incredulously.

Jesse winked at him before turning back to Kelly. "Besides, these guys could sell snow cones in January. We might as well put them to good use."

"I've got the first shift," Rio smiled dangerously. "Let's get started by making flavored lube."

The men had been trying for weeks to get them to make flavored lube and had been ignored.

Rio pulled out one of the large mixing pots and looked at Kelly and Jesse expectantly.

"Oh, God," Kelly giggled and ran a hand through her hair. She looked over at Jesse. "Don't you need him out front?"

"Nope."

Kelly watched Jesse disappear through the doorway, and then looked over to where the men gathered, taking herbs and scents out of the cabinet and sniffing them, commenting on the various scents and flavors that should be used for the lube.

It would be a long day.

"Thinking about Blade?"

Kelly blinked, pulled from her thoughts to see Jesse leaning against the counter.

Kelly shrugged, embarrassed to be caught daydreaming. "How did you know?"

Jesse pointed to where Kelly's hand stroked the choker. "You play with the choker that Blade gave you whenever you're thinking about him or when you're nervous. You played with it the whole time Ace talked about Simon."

"Really?" Kelly frowned, surprised.

"Really. You've been looking out the window, staring at Blade. Since he and Rio went out there, you've watched him until your eyes glaze over. So I figured that Blade dominated your thoughts, not nerves."

The words 'dominate' and 'Blade' in the same sentence made her heart beat faster.

"It's a little of both," she admitted, glancing around to make sure no one could hear them.

"Relax. Rio and Blade are out front and I sent Frank out for sandwiches. Spill it."

Kelly sighed. "I told Blade that I wanted him to show me the kind of sex *he* likes. You know, to be the way he usually is when he has sex with a woman, what he likes personally."

"Okay." Jesse looked puzzled. "That makes sense. You said you needed to make sure you could handle sex the way Blade wanted it. That would be the only way to find out. So what? You don't like it?"

"No. I mean yes, I like it."

"If the way your face just turned bright red is any indication, you *really* like it!"

"Okay, yes. I love it. Jesus, that man is great at sex."

Jesse frowned again. "Okay. So, what's the problem?"

Kelly glanced around again. She couldn't meet Jesse's eyes. "He wants me to be submissive. He's a *Dom,* Jesse. Remember? I don't want to be a sub!"

Kelly shifted uncomfortably. Jesse frowned, staring at her intently. "I'm not sure I understand, Kelly. I thought you said the sex was great."

"It is."

"And you and Blade care about each other, right?"

"I'm not quite sure what Blade feels for me," she admitted.

"You don't think he cares for you?"

Kelly thought about Blade's tenderness throughout the previous night. "Yes, I think he cares *something* for me. I just don't know what."

"Okay, so until you figure it out, you and Blade are getting to know each other and having a wonderful and fulfilling sex life while you're doing it. So, again, what's the problem?"

"I don't want to be a sub!"

Startled by her own outburst, Kelly spun and stalked into the back room and began pulling out the ingredients she needed to crush for her next batch of bath oil.

Jesse followed her and leaned against the countertop. "So, Blade is dominant during sex, right?"

"Yes," Kelly hissed. "He makes sure he's always in charge. That makes me a sub!"

"Ahhh." Jesse moved to the refrigerator and took out a bottle of water.

"What's that supposed to mean?" Kelly muttered irritably.

"What you don't like is the label, Kelly. By your own admission, you love Blade's dominance in the bedroom."

"Playroom," Kelly corrected absently.

"Well that sounds interesting. Some day when there's no threat of us being interrupted, I want to hear all about it. I think this little talk is going to make Clay and Rio very happy tonight. Hmm, playroom. Anyway," Jesse flicked her hand in the air, "you like what Blade does to you and he obviously likes doing it. You're just hung up on a label."

"I don't know, Jesse."

Through the window, Kelly saw Frank approaching with their lunch.

"Look," Jesse said, and turned to her, "most of the men in this town are dominant and controlling. It doesn't matter if they call themselves Doms or not. Blade doesn't expect you to be his little slave out of the playroom, does he?"

"Not so far," Kelly admitted with a shrug. "But-"

"But nothing, Kelly. You're not going to let a little thing like a label get in the way of your happiness, are you?"

"Well-"

"Honey, I don't care how big and strong or dominant he is. He cares about you. No matter what the labels are, you have more power over Blade than you think." Jesse laughed and sipped her water. "Damn, this conversation is making me hot." She started back toward the front. "I'll tell Blade and Rio that lunch is here." She paused at the doorway. "Try it, Kelly. Pay attention. You'll see just how much power you have over Blade. Make *him* lose control. You'll both love it."

Kelly watched Jesse disappear through the doorway and couldn't believe how much better she felt. Shaking Blade's control would go a long way in making her feel better about being called a submissive. The label made her feel weak and small. She'd had enough of that with Simon.

Blade walked in the back room at the same time Frank walked in with their lunch. Blade immediately sought her out, warming her all the way through.

All through lunch, he kept sending glances her way that she couldn't read.

He looked...uncomfortable? Blade? No, not Blade. Nervous? Maybe he still worried about Simon coming to town.

At Jesse's puzzled glance, Kelly shrugged.

Blade must have noticed the look that passed between the two women because when Kelly looked up, the he'd donned the cool mask once again.

Tonight she'd see if she had as much power over Blade as Jesse gave her credit for. Vowing to make Blade forget all about Simon, the way he'd done for her last night, Kelly smiled to herself and went back to her lunch.

Kelly shook with nerves by the time Sebastian pulled into the parking lot of the club. The way Blade had been acting strangely all day left her unsettled. He'd left this afternoon soon after Clay arrived.

The two men spoke briefly in the back while Jesse and Kelly helped customers in the store. By the time all the customers left, so had Blade.

Not a word of goodbye. No kiss. Nothing.

Kelly wondered all day if he still wanted to see her tonight and breathed a sigh of relief when Sebastian arrived just as the store closed.

Excitement bubbled inside her at the thought of Blade's reaction to her new wax job. She couldn't wait to see his face when he saw it.

His earlier mood still bothered her. His strange behavior all day made her realize he'd acted differently the previous night, too. Looking back, she realized he'd been almost…desperate when making love to her. He'd insisted over and over that she say his name.

Kelly frowned as she followed Sebastian into the private entrance to the club, the only entrance she could use. The main entrance could only be used by members. She followed Sebastian absently, her mind preoccupied with Blade's recent mood.

Sighing, she rubbed her forehead. She hadn't known him intimately long enough to read all his moods. He'd always been so composed with her, hiding his thoughts behind that cool mask of his.

Since they'd started having sex, she began seeing a different side of him, but she still didn't understand the way his mind ticked.

When Sebastian opened a door, Kelly blinked in surprise. She'd been so caught up in her thoughts, she hadn't realized they'd arrived. He led her into the room with a hand at her elbow, handed her an envelope and left without a word. She started into the room and came to an abrupt halt.

Sebastian had led her to the wrong room!

This one looked much larger than the one Blade had taken her to before. Her eyes widened in shock when she saw that there were a lot of apparatus here that she hadn't seen in the other room.

She looked around and saw a lot more shelves.

They were all packed full of things she'd never seen before!

Dazed, she moved to a bench and dropped her purse on it before ripping open the envelope.

Robe In Dressing Room

Kelly flipped the paper over. Nothing on the back. She searched the envelope. Nothing.

She didn't know if she should be in this room or if Sebastian made a mistake. Moving to the door, she tried the handle. Locked.

She couldn't imagine Sebastian making such a mistake, and if she *was* in the wrong room, Blade would find her soon enough. She'd better put the robe on.

Just as she turned away from the door, she heard it open and sighed in relief when Blade walked in. Smiling, she flew to him and lifted her face for his kiss.

"I knew you'd find me. Sebastian must have put me in the wrong room."

"He put you where I told him to put you."

Kelly frowned at his tone and the way he hesitated before kissing her. When she opened her mouth to ask him about it, he leaned down and captured her mouth with his.

He ate at her mouth hungrily. Heat slammed into her and she wrapped her arms around him desperately.

He lifted his head and growled. "Come with me," and pulled her into the bathroom/dressing room, closing the door behind him.

"Let me see that bare pussy."

He had her jeans undone and down to her knees before she could react. He ripped her panties off, the delicate lace no match for his strong hands.

Kneeling in front of her, he stared at her bare mound for several seconds. She could even feel the air touch her folds and felt even more exposed than she'd anticipated. Nothing blocked his view now. He could see *everything!*

Her slit flooded and she knew he would see the moisture on her folds. It felt naughty and yes, submissive to bare herself to him this way. With no small amount of surprise, she realized that baring herself to him so completely had subtly changed her mind set. She actually *felt* more submissive and vulnerable than before.

With his experience, he had to know that, proving once again he understood her body's responses better than she did.

She stood, frozen in place when he reached for her. His hand shook, she noted in surprise, as he touched her. She gripped his shoulder to steady herself, absently noticing his tension. She sucked in a breath at the first touch of his hand on her bare skin.

"Beautiful," he breathed as he traced her folds with his fingertips. "I have to taste you."

When his mouth replaced his fingers, Kelly couldn't prevent a moan, fighting to remain upright.

"Oh, Blade. It's too much." She groaned when his hot tongue slid through her slit. The way too sensitive feel of his tongue sent her spiraling far too soon. His tongue felt even more intimate on her with nothing barring his way.

Dangerously close to coming, she groaned when Blade lifted his head. He stood and regarded her steadily, nodding in satisfaction.

Why wouldn't he finish her off?

He wanted to make her wait again!

His heart raced under her hands, which slid to his chest and she could see his own control slip.

"Get undressed. Put on the robe."

"But, Blade," Kelly began, but he took her hands in his, removing them from his chest. He stepped back, putting distance between them.

"Do you trust me, Kelly? Really trust me?"

Kelly frowned up at him. "Of course."

"Then do as I told you and go out to the playroom."

"Why aren't we in *your* playroom?"

Kelly watched, confused and a little frightened, when Blade's face tightened. His strange behavior lately really put her on edge. Nothing he did made sense to her anymore.

"This is the club playroom. Do as I told you."

Kelly frowned after him as he stalked out of the room.

She needed to get to the bottom of this. She'd make him tell her what the hell had changed him.

She quickly finished undressing and donned the white robe, loving the feel of silk against her skin. For some reason he didn't want her to walk out naked, so she checked to make sure it covered her completely.

Hopefully that wouldn't last too long.

Noticing how pink her cheeks had become, she smiled at her reflection and hurried out, so Blade could finish what he'd started. Still smiling, she walked into the playroom.

She came to an abrupt halt, her smile falling when she saw Royce waited for her instead of Blade. Gathering her robe more firmly around her, she looked around in confusion.

"Hello, Royce. What are you doing here? Where's Blade? He didn't tell you we were using this room?"

"Yes, Blade told me you were here. Blade left."

"Left?" Kelly gaped at him incredulously.

For the first time she noticed what Royce wore. Black leather pants hugged his trim hips and the white shirt, plain except for the flowing sleeves, contrasted sharply with his dark complexion.

He looked dangerous, and very much a Dom.

The look on his face nearly stopped her heart. She'd seen it on Blade's countless times. The warm welcoming look he usually gave her had disappeared. It had been composed into the cool look of a dominate, controlled man.

When he shifted, she automatically took a step back and for the first time she noticed that he wore a strange belt around his waist. She gulped when she saw what hung from it.

A WHIP!?

"Where's Blade?" she whispered frantically.

"I told you. He left."

When Royce took another step toward her, she again stepped back, intending to run back into the dressing room for her clothes. Instead she ran straight into a rock hard wall. She gasped in surprise and horror when she saw she'd run into King, who'd blocked her path.

Kelly grasped her robe tighter around her and stumbled away, keeping them both in sight.

"What's going on? I want Blade."

King, dressed similarly to Royce, spoke for the first time.

"Blade left you here with us."

Kelly shook her head in confusion. "I don't understand. Why?"

Royce raised a brow, the mannerism so identical to Blade's, it made her stomach drop.

"He left you with us, so we can play together."

"No." Kelly's voice came out a thin whisper. "He wouldn't do that."

"It's okay, Kelly. You have his permission. He did it for you. Didn't you say you wanted to learn if you could give up control?"

"He told you that?"

"Of course," Royce replied silkily. "He wants to help you. King and I like to share. Wouldn't you like to be able to give up control to two Doms? It would be like having two Blades. Wouldn't you like to experience that kind of pleasure?"

"No," Kelly shook her head, holding out her hand as though to ward them off.

"Think of how good we can make you feel." King's rough voice lowered softly as if to calm her even as he took another step closer. "Royce and I will make you come so many times, you'll lose count," he promised darkly, stepping even closer.

Kelly continued to back away from them, circling a padded table and moving around it, so it stood between her and the men.

"Isn't that what you need, Kelly?" Royce purred. "King and I will make you feel so good. Now, come on, honey, take off the robe like a good girl. I don't want to start off our time together by spanking you."

He moved close and lowered his face to within inches of hers. "But maybe that's what you need. Would you like that, honey? Would you like being draped over my lap, so I can make that gorgeous ass of yours red?"

"Please, no!" It came out as a thin whimper.

"Come on, honey. Open the robe and let King and I have those luscious breasts."

The thought of either of them touching her filled Kelly with revulsion. Both gorgeous and breathtaking in their dominance, she still couldn't stand the thought of either of them touching her.

She wanted only Blade.

But he left her with them.

Impossible. He'd said she belonged to him.

"Blade left me here with you?" She couldn't believe it.

Royce smiled darkly. "Obviously."

"Blade knows you're both in here with me?"

"Absolutely." King answered coolly. He reached for the belt of her robe. "Give me the robe."

"Blade gave me to you?" Kelly croaked hoarsely. "He said you could touch me, that you could, you know?"

King had moved around her and closed in from behind, pulling her back against his chest with an arm around her waist.

It felt like she'd been pulled back against a tree trunk. She fought wildly until she realized her struggles did nothing but loosen her robe.

She whimpered. "Please don't do this," she begged. Tears ran down her face and she wanted nothing more than to get away from them.

"Blade said you want to let go of control, to see if you can enjoy sex again." King murmured against her ear, "It's only sex, honey. Let Royce and I make you feel good."

"It's not only sex!" she screamed tearfully, nearly hysterical now. "I only want Blade!"

Royce ran a finger down her neck and traced the opening of her robe. "I don't understand, honey. You said you wanted Blade to teach you to enjoy sex while giving up control. We can do that for you, honey."

"I lied," Kelly whimpered, and broke.

She felt herself being lifted and folded in King's arms as sobs racked her body. When he sat in a chair, Kelly tried to push from his lap, but he held onto her as easily as he would a child.

"What do you mean, you lied?" he asked softly.

"I t-told Blade that s-so he w-would make l-love to me," she hiccuped. "I d-didn't want him t-to know."

"Know what, honey?" King stroked her back soothingly.

Kelly couldn't answer, her throat so clogged with tears it made speech impossible.

Blade didn't want her.

All her dreams of having a life with him came crashing down around her. Before, at least she'd had some hope. Now she had none. Why did she ever think he could feel something for her?

Oh, God, it hurt!

She'd never hurt like this before, not even when Simon did his worst to her.

Simon!

He'd already tried to bring her down and she'd learned to be strong. She'd be damned before she let Blade bring her down again!

To hell with him. She had to get out of here.

Wiping her eyes on her sleeve, she looked up at King.

"Let me go."

"You love Blade. Don't you, honey?"

"No! I hate him! Let me up!"

King smiled and opened his arms, allowing her to scramble out of them.

She stood, tightening her robe more securely around her and headed for the other room to get her clothes.

And froze in her tracks.

Blade stood just inside the room, looking pale and shaken. Her heart leaped at the sight of him before she tamped it down.

Bastard!

She watched as Royce and King left the room, slapping Blade on the shoulder as they passed.

Blade never acknowledged them, his eyes never leaving hers.

"I'm sorry, love. So sorry."

She wouldn't let his stricken look affect her. Hardening her heart against the anguish in his eyes, she gathered herself, determined not to let him see how he'd shattered her heart.

"Go fuck yourself!" Kelly screamed at him and stalked into the dressing room, slamming the door behind her.

Chapter Nine

Blade winced as the door slammed and knew he'd made the biggest mistake of his life.

The control he prided himself on had vanished. Dealing with the woman he loved had him floundering just as badly as the next man.

He'd prayed that Kelly loved him, but had underestimated the extent of her response to Royce and King.

He'd stupidly assumed she'd do one of two things. Either she'd take Royce and King up on their offer, which would have nearly killed him, or she'd get pissed off and tell them no. If she'd accepted, he would have known he'd misjudged and would have to try to get over her. If she'd gotten mad, well, he would have loved the chance to deal with her fiery temper.

But neither had happened.

He hadn't factored in her response to thinking he'd given her to someone else or his friends determination to get her to admit her feelings.

He'd hurt her, and it devastated him.

Christ, what a mess.

He had only himself to blame. Royce and King had done what he'd asked them to and he should have known that they wouldn't quit until she'd admitted her feelings. They'd both told him repeatedly that she loved him and knew he didn't quite believe it.

The club playroom had hidden cameras for safety reasons. He's watched from his office, his hands clenched into fists the entire time. When she'd started crying, he ran out the door and down the hall before he'd even realized it.

Standing there, just inside the door, frozen to the spot, he watched King comfort her, and wanted to yank her out of his friend's arms. Royce had held him back.

"You wanted the truth." Royce's whispered reminder had kept him silent. "You won't be satisfied until you hear it for yourself."

When he heard the bathroom door open, he straightened. Kelly appeared, dressed, her eyes red and swollen, and he wanted to pull her into his arms and hold her. But the hard look in her eyes told him his touch wouldn't be welcome.

She'd never looked at him that way before and it cut him to the quick. When she started to walk past him, he reached out and touched her arm, wincing when she pulled away.

"Kelly, love, please let me explain."

"Red light. There, happy. You were right. You finally got me to say it. Now get your fucking hands off me! Open the door."

When Blade just stood there, Kelly thought he would refuse. She needed to get away from him before she embarrassed herself by crying again.

She was surprised when he nodded.

"I'll walk you back to your room."

"No. I'm going home."

Blade shook his head. "Not until Simon is caught. You have to stay here."

"No, I don't want to be around you right now."

"If you go back to your apartment, I'm going with you. If you stay here, I promise I'll leave you alone until you're ready to talk to me."

Kelly eyed him warily. "I don't believe you."

"That's the best offer you're going to get. I want you to stay here where you'll be safe. If you want me to leave you alone for now, I will."

"I do."

"For now," he growled. "After you've settled down, you and I are going to have this out."

Kelly forced herself not to weaken at the dejected look on his face or how his body language showed defeat.

Nodding again, he moved to the door and unlocked it.

Kelly stayed in her room at the club, only venturing out to go to work. Sebastian waited outside to take her to *Indulgences* every day and either Clay or Rio brought her back every night.

She knew they'd spoken to Blade because they never mentioned him, only looked at her compassionately when they dropped her off. She refused to discuss it with Jesse and had stormed out once when Jesse wouldn't let it drop.

Rio had found her at the diner and brought her back, and they didn't mention Blade's name again.

Royce and King kept trying to talk to her, but she carefully avoided them.

She hadn't seen or heard from Blade since he'd led her to her room.

She missed him so much she couldn't stand it. She'd lost weight and she had circles under her eyes from not sleeping.

She needed him.

When the day of the Fourth of July picnic finally arrived, Kelly showered and dressed. She'd talk to Blade today. She needed to get everything out in the open and let him tell her why he'd done what he had. She couldn't stand this distance between them and she wanted to hear him explain.

The businesses in town closed for the day. Kelly had watched the preparations all week from her window.

Looking out the window, she saw Blade coming out of the back of the club, heading toward the picnic grounds. She ran to catch him.

She ran down the stairs, not wanting to wait for the elevator. At the bottom, she turned, almost running over Sebastian in her haste.

"Where are you going in such a hurry?"

Kelly didn't slow down. "I've got to catch Blade."

She caught a glimpse of the butler's smile as she turned and ran out the back door. Looking around, she didn't see Blade and started to walk to the festivities, searching everywhere for his tall form.

What was that?

She heard it again. It sounded like a ...groan? She slowed her steps and moved in the direction it came from. There were several cars and trucks already here as people had started setting up their booths.

When she saw the tip of a black boot, she felt an icy dread go through her. She quickly moved to the other side of the truck and gasped when she saw Blade lying on the ground.

"Blade!"

She ran to him, skidding on her knees as she landed beside him. He was out cold! When she tried to lift his head, he groaned again and she felt a sticky wetness on her hand. When she moved her hand to look at it, her heart stopped.

Blood!

She opened her mouth to scream for help when a hand clamped over it.

"I've come for what's mine, slut."

Simon!

She'd forgotten all about him!

"Let's go. If you scream, I'll shoot lover boy." He took his hand from her mouth slowly as though afraid she would disobey him.

She turned to look up at him and saw the insanity in his eyes. Her own widened when she saw that he had a gun.

"Why are you here?" she asked inanely. Her mind screamed only one thing.

Blade was hurt!

"I told you, bitch. I came for what's mine. You thought you could get away from me. Never! *You're mine!*"

When Simon yanked her up by her hair, she dropped Blade's head as he jerked her to her feet. She heard Blade moan again and saw Simon point his gun at him.

"NO!" She screamed and tried to grab his arm. He backhanded her across the face and she tasted blood.

He pulled her along behind him. She slid several times on the gravel as he yanked her along. "You're coming with me. I'm going to teach you a lesson you'll never forget."

She'd never seen him this far gone before and knew she may not survive if he managed to take her. He dragged her through the grounds and around the parked cars. She dug in her heels but couldn't stop him. Insanity had given him more strength than she could ever remember him having.

He acted like a madman as he dragged her, kicking and screaming through the rows of cars and trucks, stopping periodically to hit her again. He called her names, his eyes darting wildly. Spittle shot out of his mouth as his threats and name calling continued. She'd never seen him so enraged!

Scared for both Blade and herself, she fought like never before. She tried to dig her heels in, but found it impossible on the gravel surface. Their combined shouts became so loud, she'd hoped someone would hear them. But with all the noise around, she worried that no one would.

Her struggles seemed to madden him further. "You fucking bitch! You let a Dom fuck you! I'll show you I can dominate you better than him!" He punched her in the jaw and she saw stars.

Her feet dragged as the world spun dizzily around her. Simon half dragged, half carried her to an old truck parked at the end of the grounds. He threw her unceremoniously into the passenger seat and slammed the door behind her.

She had to get out!

Her fingers fumbled for the door handle as she watched Simon come around the front of the truck.

Suddenly Blade came flying out of nowhere and tackled Simon. She heard a gunshot and suddenly several men surrounded the truck.

She saw Ace and his deputies in front of the truck, but she couldn't see what was going on. The men all scrambled and she heard a scuffle, followed by cursing and grunts. Ace hauled Simon to his feet. He looked even worse than he had moments ago.

The truck door opened and she would have fallen out if King hadn't caught her. He lifted her out carefully, his hold on her incredibly gentle.

"Oh, honey. You're all beat up again."

Her eye burned and she could taste blood. "Blade." She started to struggle.

"Okay, honey. Take it easy. I'll take you over."

She could see the paramedics rushing over with the gurney. Thank God they'd been here for the picnic as a precaution.

When she saw Blade, everything inside her went numb. He grimaced as he stood, one side of his shirt soaked with blood.

So much blood!

When she saw him struggle against Clay and Royce, her heart started beating again.

"Let me down."

She gave King no choice as she struggled harder to get to Blade. She heard King's curse as he finally released her.

"Kelly?"

Blade's voice sounded thin and weak and she'd never heard anything so wonderful in her life.

"Oh, Blade!" She reached past Clay to touch his face, staring at the blood all over him. "You're hurt. Did he *shoot* you?"

"Just nicked me. Oh, love. I'm sorry I couldn't get to you faster. Look at you. You're all beat up again."

Then he passed out.

"No!" Kelly fisted her hands in his shirt. "Blade!" She screamed and cried as King pulled her off and into his arms again.

"He's okay, honey. He passed out. I don't know how he stayed conscious as long as he did. Probably to see you're okay."

Clay came to her side after they'd loaded Blade onto the gurney. "I'm sure he's got a concussion, but he'll be fine, honey. Let's get you to the ambulance and you can ride with him."

Kelly had been treated, with Jesse and Nat by her side and came out to the waiting room to find it packed.

"It's all my fault," Kelly told Ace for about the twentieth time as she leaned against Jesse, who sat beside her.

"You can't blame yourself, honey," Ace said yet again. "Simon is the one responsible."

"I'd forgotten all about him. I saw Blade leave and went after him to talk to him."

She thought of all the blood on Blade. "He won't die, will he?"

Royce and King had told her what happened that day in the playroom, explaining to her that Blade loved her but couldn't be sure that she loved him, not just what he could make her feel.

"If one of us had touched you intimately, he would have broken off our hands and fed them to us," Royce had told her.

"Of course he's not going to die." Nat reached out and touched Kelly's arm. "Blade's going to be fine. You have to be strong. He's going to need you with him to get better."

Kelly stood and started pacing, "I'm going to make sure he recovers quickly. Then I'm going to put him back in the hospital again."

She got so caught up in her ranting that she didn't pay much attention when Clay led her back to the chair and made her sit.

"He's an idiot," she grunted and stood to pace again. "How could he think I didn't love him?" She looked at Jesse.

"How much longer? He's been in surgery for hours." She began pacing again. "How could he not know that I loved him? I'm going to take him to his playroom and hit him on the head with one of his paddles."

A grinning King led her back to the chair this time and settled her while she continued to rant.

"He thinks he's so smart, but..."

Kelly stopped when she saw the surgeon and Dr. Hansen, Desire's town doctor walk in, and jumped up to run to them.

The men sighed as they kept up with her.

"How is he?" Kelly asked fearfully.

Everyone breathed a sigh of relief when the surgeon grinned.

"He's a tough son of...he's tough." He shook his head. "The bullet missed all his vital organs. It glanced off his ribs, broke a couple of them, but he's going to be fine. He's got a concussion, so his head is going to hurt like the dickens for a couple of days, then he can go home."

Kelly didn't feel her knees give out, but Royce and King grabbed her with muffled curses and led her back to the chair.

"When can we see him?" Kelly asked the surgeon.

"He'll be in recovery for a while. You can probably see him in two or three hours. I'll have the nurse let you know."

Everyone thanked the surgeon as he left and started firing questions at Dr. Hansen, who'd stayed behind.

Dr. Hansen raised his hands. "I'll answer all your questions. Let's all sit down first."

When everyone settled, Dr. Hansen addressed them like a teacher with a classroom full of students.

"The way the bullet hit, it broke two of his ribs and cracked two more. He's going to be sore for a while." He looked around the room, his eyes lingering on Jesse. "A lot of you have had broken ribs, so you know what I'm talking about."

He smiled when Clay and Rio both reached out to touch Jesse as though assuring themselves that she was okay even though her ribs had healed weeks ago.

"Did I understand right? He stepped *into* the bullet?"

"Dove, actually," Royce muttered.

Dr. Hansen shook his head. "The bullet hit at such a strange angle. If he'd taken it straight on, his injuries would have been a lot worse."

Several comments and heartfelt sighs could be heard around the room before the doctor continued.

"He should be able to go home in a few days. We have to keep an eye on the concussion. The stitches will be sore, as will the ribs. He's on antibiotics, but he'll still be monitored for infection. He'll be bedridden for a little while, and he's going to be a pain."

He looked at Kelly, who sat with Royce and King. "He came to briefly when he was brought in. He asked repeatedly for you three. I think to keep him calm, the three of you need to go in as soon as he's out of recovery."

Kelly nodded, unable to speak and gripped King's hand tighter.

"Absolutely," Royce nodded.

"We'll be right here," King added.

"Good. I didn't expect any less. I expect one of you will see to him when he's released?"

"I'll be there with him." Kelly looked at Jesse. "I need…"

"Absolutely. Between Brittany, Katy, and I, we'll be fine. You just take care of Blade, *and yourself*," she added sternly.

"I'm available, too." Nat came forward. "You know I love being at the shop. You don't have to worry about anything except you and Blade getting better."

"King and I will be there, too." Royce smiled for the first time in hours. "If I know Blade, he's going to be a bear. But, between the three of us, we should be able to handle him."

He frowned at Kelly. "As soon as we see Blade, we'll take you back to the club. You need to go to bed."

Two hours later, Kelly, with Royce and King flanking her, was led to Blade's room. He'd awakened and asked for them, finally yelling at the nurses and being completely uncooperative until she left to get them.

Kelly paused outside the room and took a deep calming breath, bracing herself for seeing Blade hooked up to the tubes and monitors Dr. Hansen had warned them about. Royce and King stopped beside her and watched as she gathered her strength around her like a cloak before she stepped forward.

"It took you long enough," Blade rumbled as soon as they walked into the room.

"Well hello to you, too. We were having an orgy in the waiting room." Kelly carefully kept her fear from showing. "What kind of idiot tackles a man with a gun?"

"You weren't part of an orgy. You won't let anyone but *me* touch you," he told her smugly. "What took you so long?"

"The nurse just came to get us. She said you were being rude and uncooperative. You're not even supposed to have visitors yet. They sent us up to deal with you."

"Deal with me? Wait until I get out of this bed. Then we'll see who deals with who," he growled at her weakly, but his eyes shot sparks at her.

"Get over here and let me see you," he ordered and turned to his friends. "Is she okay?"

"*She* can answer for herself. I'm fine. I'm not an idiot like some people."

"An idiot?" Blade sighed and closed his eyes. "I guess I am when it comes to you."

He stretched out his hand and she hurriedly put hers in it, loving the ability to touch him again.

He rubbed her hand with his thumb, his eyes holding hers. "I needed to know if it was me or just sex you wanted," Blade told her softly. They'd both forgotten the other men were in the room. "Now that I know you love me, the agreement is off."

Kelly felt her stomach drop and she narrowed her eyes at him. "What do you mean, the agreement's off?"

"What agreement?" Royce asked, but they ignored him.

"No more six week agreement," Blade warned. "You're mine now, and you're going to stay mine. You're going to learn what's it's like to be my woman if I have to punish you every day."

"My ass!" Kelly shouted back.

"Oh, your ass is very much a part of my plans," Blade told her silkily.

"What makes you think I'm going to put up with someone who wants me to be their puppet?"

"Puppet?" Blade asked in disbelief. "Who said anything about wanting you to be my puppet?"

Kelly began muttering to both Blade and herself, much to the amusement of both Royce and King, who'd pulled up chairs to watch in comfort.

"If you think," Kelly began, "that I'm going to do what you say, you're delusional."

"A nice red ass will fix that," Blade told her and frowned at her when she ignored him.

"I'm nobody's puppet. It doesn't matter how much I love you, I'm not going to ever again let a man run my life, especially one stupid enough to run into a bullet."

"If you call me stupid one more time…"

Kelly ignored him and stopped pacing to look at him. "Thank you, by the way, but don't *ever* do that again!"

Royce and King saw Blade smile when Kelly admitted she loved him, but it quickly turned to a frown when he raised a brow at her lecturing command.

Wishing he had popcorn, Royce settled back and got comfortable, glancing up when Ace walked in.

Kelly continued to lecture Blade on his stupid behavior, like jumping into bullets and setting her up with his friends.

When Ace shot a questioning look at King, he just smiled and put a finger over his lips. Neither Blade nor Kelly seemed to know Ace had come into the room as their argument continued.

Ace shrugged and leaned against the wall, soon becoming part of the rapt audience.

"I don't understand you at all." Kelly continued her pacing at the foot of Blade's bed. "One minute you're trying to give me away to your buddies, the next you're jumping in front of a bullet for me!"

"But you love me. You said so. And neither Royce nor King would have touched you."

Ace raised a brow at that but wisely said nothing.

"What kind of idiot are you?" Kelly demanded. "If I just wanted sex, I could get that anywhere."

"Like hell!"

"But if you think just because I love you, I'm going to let you boss me around, you're crazy."

Kelly stopped her pacing and poked her finger at him. "You have to love me, too."

"I do."

"If you don't love me now, then I'm just going to have to make you."

"I do."

"While you're home recuperating, you're going to be at my mercy for a change, and I'm not going to put up with …what did you say?"

Blade held out his hand. "Come here."

Kelly moved closer and put her hand in Blade's.

"I said, I do love you, minx."

"*Oh, Blade.*" Kelly leaned forward, careful of his injuries and rained kisses all over his face.

"You love me?"

"Absolutely." He sobered. "Are you really all right?"

"Of course." She leaned in and touched her lips softly to his. "You saved me."

"If you ever scare me like that again, your ass is going to be so red you won't be able to sit down for a week!"

Kelly laughed. "Yeah, yeah, yeah. Don't forget, you're flat on your back. You're in no position to threaten me."

Blade grinned. "Yeah, but when I've recovered and I get *you* flat on your back again…"

"Promises, promises," Kelly laughed in delight. Blade really was going to be okay. He loved her. She'd never been so happy, black eye and all.

For the first time she noticed Ace leaning against the wall, grinning. All of a sudden, she remembered Royce and King. Seeing that they wore similar grins, she blushed.

"Sorry. I forgot you were here."

King chuckled. "That's okay, honey. We enjoyed the show, especially the way you told Blade off. I've never seen that happen before."

Kelly raised her chin. "You'll be seeing that a lot. I'm not going to let him, owww!"

She rubbed her bottom where Blade had pinched it, scowling at him when he chuckled.

"Just because I love you doesn't mean you're going to get away with sassing me."

"You're going to be at my mercy while you're getting better. We'll have a lot of time to discuss your bossiness."

"I'll keep track of all punishable offenses and make good on every one of them as soon as we're married."

"Married?! We never talked about getting married."

"I know, but you are going to marry me aren't you?"

"Yeah, I guess I am. I love you, you know?" Kelly looked at the love shining from his eyes and the underlying fear.

"I know, love," he slurred and she knew talking had worn him out.

Kelly patted his arm. "You rest. I'll be in the waiting room."

"No. I need to talk to Ace, then King and Royce. Then they're going to take you home. You need some rest and I'm sure the medicine they gave you for pain will be wearing off soon. Now give me my kiss."

"What kiss?"

Chapter Ten

The next two days Kelly spent her time at the hospital with Blade. He had a constant stream of visitors coming through to see for themselves that he would recover.

The day he'd been brought in, when she'd left his room to go out to the waiting room, she'd walked up to Jesse and promptly burst into tears, the dam breaking.

"What happened?" Jesse had asked anxiously. "Is Blade okay?"

"He's okay. I love him. He loves me. We're getting married!"

Jesse, Nat, and Rachel had squealed in delight while the men looked on in amused indulgence as the women began to make plans.

Rio laughed in relief. "Even flat on his back and doped up, Blade manages to run the show."

When Royce and King had come out to join them, King went immediately to Kelly and hugged her. "You did great in there. I was afraid you would fall apart. Instead, you argued with him and challenged him. That will get him out of that bed faster than anything." He smiled teasingly. "He definitely has some plans for you."

"You argued with him?" Jesse asked incredulously.

"I just asked him what kind of idiot jumped in front of a bullet. One thing led to another and before I knew how it happened, I'd admitted I loved him." She frowned.

"Then," Royce added, grinning at her, "she tells him that he's not bossing her around anymore and that she's not going to be his puppet."

Kelly felt her cheeks flush when everyone laughed. She glared at Royce as he continued.

"She also threatened to deal with his bossiness while he was flat on his back."

"But for now," Royce took her arm, "we have strict orders to take you back to the club and see that you eat something and get a good night's sleep."

Since then, Kelly had spent her time with Blade and the two of them had talked quite a bit. She became surer than ever that she'd made the right choice in agreeing to marry him.

Today he would go home. Since moving around still hurt him, Royce and King had come to help him.

His mood wasn't the best. He hated being so weak and sore, and he took it out on everyone around him which made Kelly feel guilty as hell. When he saw it, his attitude became a little better and he assured her repeatedly that none of this had been her fault.

Simon had been arrested and wouldn't be getting out of jail for a very long time. They were doing a psychiatric evaluation, and no one thought he'd pass.

When they finally got Blade to his apartment at the club, and into bed, his eyes closed as soon as his head touched the pillow. Kelly watched as he fell asleep, his face unusually pale, and adjusted the light blanket around him.

Settling herself on the nearby sofa, she picked up one of the books Jesse had brought her. Some time later, Kelly closed the book and blew out a breath. Wow. This book was hot! Her panties had even gotten wet by the time she'd finished it.

If only Blade wasn't out of commission!

Where did Jesse get this stuff? Vowing to ask and start her own collection, Kelly smiled and looked up to check on Blade, to find him watching her.

"Good book?"

"Oh, yeah."

"You're flushed. Was it that good?"

Kelly stood and went over to sit next to him on the bed. "Are you hungry?"

"Yeah, that's what woke me up. I need something besides hospital food. I have to get my energy back up to deal with you and make whatever you just read look like child's play."

The look in his eyes made her pulse race and she laughed. "I'll go tell the chef. He's been waiting to see what you felt like eating."

"Tell him to fix me a steak and a salad. Did you eat?"

"No. I wanted to wait for you."

"Give me the phone. Push two."

When Kelly did as he asked, Blade ordered steak, salad, and a baked potato for each of them.

"You need to get your energy up, too, for what I have in store for you when I'm back on my feet." He pursed his sensuous lips. "It appears I have a woman who believes she can get away with sassing me."

Pure lust raced through her. She sat looking at him for several seconds, trying to get it under control.

When Kelly took the phone to hang it up, Blade began unbuttoning her shirt one handed.

"Blade," she moaned. "Stop. You can't."

"I'm injured and bored and you're supposed to take care of me."

Watching his handsome face an idea formed and the flare of lust reappeared with a vengeance. She smiled mischievously. After all, how often would she have Blade helpless?

His eyes narrowed and she looked away, not wanting him to know what she'd planned. "I'm going to go lock the door."

"Hurry up," he growled when she left the bed.

After locking the door, Kelly sauntered back to the foot of the bed where Blade couldn't reach her. She finished unbuttoning her shirt, watching his face the entire time.

He carefully schooled his features, showing only cool disinterest, and she had to bite her lip to keep from smiling.

Let's see how long he could keep that composure.

Dropping her shirt to the floor, she cupped her lace covered breasts and, noting the tenting of the light covers, she reached for the snap of her jeans. She slowly undid them, lowering the zipper a tooth at a time. Challenging Blade this way turned her on so much, she hoped she could continue. She'd never done a striptease before and she loved it.

She could see that Blade loved it, too. The cool mask on his face was in sharp contrast to the growing size of the tenting of the covers.

"Come here."

Kelly blithely ignored Blade's command and slowly worked her jeans down her legs and stepped out of them. Standing in only her pink bra and thong, one of the many sets she'd recently purchased from Rachel, Kelly again cupped her breasts as though offering them to Blade.

"Come here!"

Undoing the front clasp of the bra, Kelly let the straps fall and turned her back to Blade, watching him seductively over her shoulder.

She deliberately wiggled her ass at him, watching as his eyes followed the movement. She let the bra fall to the floor. With her hands covering her breasts, she turned back to face him.

"I said come here!" he growled.

Every time he ordered the harsh command, his voice got deeper and more menacing. Kelly loved it! She knew he'd never get away with this, which made her even hotter. She knew this kind of thing would rack up those punishments he talked about.

She couldn't wait.

Kelly ran her hands over her breasts, throwing her head back in abandon as she lightly pinched her nipples, knowing Blade watched every move.

Moaning, she continued to play with them, opening her eyes to watch Blade.

The tent had gotten larger.

"I told you to come here."

Wow! That sounded really cold. And she had gotten really wet.

Her inhibitions flew out the window when she saw Blade's reaction to her play. Smiling at him daringly, she took her middle finger into her mouth, wetting it, and drawing it down her body until it disappeared into her panties.

Blade's eyes flared as he followed the motion.

"Come here *right now!*"

Kelly ran her finger through her slit, moaning as she fingered her clit. Turning her back to him again, she pulled her hand out of her panties and hooked a thumb on each side, bending at the waist as she lowered them to the floor.

"Get the fuck over here right now!"

Straightening, Kelly turned and leaned over the foot of the bed, placing a hand on either side of Blade's feet.

"Did you want something?" Kelly asked innocently.

"Do you have any idea just how many punishments you're in for?" he asked coldly, while his eyes glittered with heat.

"Was I bad?" Kelly asked innocently, enjoying herself immensely.

When she saw the way his cock jumped beneath the covers, she knew Blade enjoyed this just as much as she did.

He nodded grimly. "You've been *very* bad. Now come here!"

Kelly yanked the covers down before Blade could stop her, exposing his naked form to her hungry gaze.

Even with the belt holding his ribs in place and the gauze bandage surrounded by bruises, he looked scrumptious.

"Let me beg for forgiveness," Kelly smiled coyly and bent to kiss his feet.

She kissed and nibbled and licked her way to his knees, smiling to herself when his cock came to full attention.

"You're in serious need of discipline," Blade said through clenched teeth.

She sighed in mock sadness. "I'm afraid it's hopeless. I just can't be good. Maybe you should give up on me."

"Not a chance. Come here."

Hiding her smile, she gave his thighs her full attention, moving from one to the other until she reached the full sack between them.

"Please forgive me."

"Not until you've been punished for each and every infraction. *Come here!*"

"No." Kelly felt Blade's hands in her hair tighten when she ran her tongue over his sack.

He hissed, then groaned as she licked his tight sack all over. "Damn it, Kelly. Come up here."

"No."

She heard him hiss when she ran her tongue up the length of his cock. Careful to keep her weight off of him, she lowered her mouth over him and took him as deeply as she could.

When he growled and tried to lift her head, she closed her teeth on him lightly in warning.

"You are going to be *severely* punished for this." He ground out menacingly.

Kelly thrilled at his dark threat and sucked him more determinedly, using her tongue on him the way she knew he liked.

His thighs tightened under her hands. Moans rumbled deep in his throat, exciting her even more. Determined to give him pleasure and snap that control of his, she sucked harder, using her tongue on the sensitive underside relentlessly.

"Damn it, Kelly. You are, fuck, definitely going to pay for this. How did you learn, ah, fuck." He growled as he came, shooting his seed into her throat. She swallowed on him, eliciting even more groans.

Smiling, she continued to lick him with long, smooth strokes, meeting his eyes as she dropped a kiss on the head and sat back on her heels. Lowering her head, she adopted a submissive pose as she raised her eyes. "Now am I forgiven?"

She noticed that Blade's lips twitched before he firmed them.

"You disobeyed me over and over. Do you know how many times I told you to come here and yet you still haven't?"

"No."

"Ten times! You either ignored me or flat out told me no. *Then* you took my cock into your mouth without permission, and when I said 'no', you still didn't listen."

She shrugged. "I wanted to make you feel better."

"And you keep interrupting me while I'm scolding you!"

Kelly bit her lip to keep from smiling.

Blade's eyes narrowed dangerously. "When I'm fully recovered, you're going to pay dearly for your insolence."

Kelly smiled serenely and nodded. "Yes, but I don't care. You love me. I was so sad when I thought you only wanted sex. I thought you couldn't love someone who stood up to you."

She licked her finger deliberately. "You made me feel again and I can't go back to what I was, not even for you."

Blade's eyes followed the movement of her hand as she reached down and parted her folds, using her slick finger to rub her clit. With the other, she plucked a nipple.

Blade's eyes darken with need as his cock again sprang to life. "Come here, love."

"Mmm," Kelly threw her head back in abandon. Touching herself like this for Blade's pleasure turned her on big time.

"COME. HERE. NOW!"

Kelly met his eyes, and smirked. "Beg me."

She was totally unprepared for the extent of his reaction. His face darkened and tightened, the true master and she froze in both fascination and apprehension.

Uh oh. Time to retreat.

Before she could act, his foot nudged her from behind, toppling her next to him. Somehow, he caught both her wrists in one large hand. His heavily muscled leg moved to cover both of hers before she could avoid it.

She couldn't move for fear of hurting him, but the look on his face made her stomach clench. She'd gone too far!

He leaned down slowly, grimacing as his ribs protested, until his nose almost touched hers. He reached out and pinched a pebbled nipple.

"You have one month. One month to find the dress you're going to be married in. One month to do all you have to do to get ready to get married."

His fingers tightened on her nipple and Kelly felt the pull of it all the way to her clit.

"You have one month to prepare yourself. We're going away for a two week honeymoon, during which you'll receive all the punishments you're accumulating and learn once and for all to obey me!"

Kelly met his gaze head on. "I love you so much."

He smiled tenderly. "I love you, too, baby." His look became all male arrogance. "But you're still going to pay.

Kelly's giggle turned into a moan when his hand wandered. "Promises, promises."

Chapter Eleven

Blade grinned as he carried the tray to his bedroom. He'd already become addicted to Kelly's softness cuddled against him through the night and couldn't wait to get back to her.

With the weeks of recovery behind him, he looked forward to marrying Kelly tomorrow and spending the next two weeks alone with her. She'd been with him throughout his recovery, taking care of him, teasing him, tormenting him, and he couldn't wait to take his revenge.

And to show her just how much he loved her.

When he'd woken earlier, he'd ached to roll onto her exquisite softness, move between those lush thighs, and relieve the raging erection her nude form had inspired.

She'd been sleeping so peacefully, though, curled trustingly against him, that he didn't want to disturb her. He'd worn her out, he thought with no small amount of satisfaction. The previous evening had worn them both out and he'd slept better than he had in years.

His grin softened when he thought about how the hand on his chest had curled when he'd lifted it to press his lips against her palm, as though to hold his kiss. That reaction had touched him deeply as did the way she'd gathered his pillow close while he'd showered and dressed.

He'd let her sleep while he left to take care of some business before their honeymoon. He'd left a note for her to call the kitchen when she woke up and her breakfast would be brought up.

A brief inquiry to the kitchen staff told him she hadn't yet called down, so he'd had them prepare a tray for him to deliver himself.

He'd rushed through his obligations to free himself for the next two weeks. He wanted nothing to distract him from his bride on their honeymoon.

Royce and King had both taunted him over the last few weeks when they saw how Kelly provoked him. Every time she had, Blade had seen her confidence in herself build. They both enjoyed it and he knew they would both enjoy it when he punished her naughty behavior.

His partners had also noticed the change in her and had commented more than once on her glowing happiness. Then they threatened to strap him to his own table in his own playroom for Kelly's enjoyment.

"It would take both of you to do that," Blade answered with a grin. "I don't need your help with my woman. I'm perfectly capable of mastering my woman on my own. Not like the two of you."

King threw a ball of paper at him. "We share because we want to, not because either of us needs help." He threw another ball of paper which hit Blade in the chest.

Blade picked up the paper when it landed on his desk and grinned. They'd bantered about this many times before. "Sure you do. That's what you keep telling me. But both of you are too soft. You'd never be able to get a woman to obey you. It would take both of you to give a woman the kind of pleasure I can give."

"Soft?" Royce wadded up a ball of paper and threw it at him. "Women beg for us and you know it. How many times have they knocked on the door, looking for King and me?"

Blade's lips twitched when he thought about the number of times that had happened. He threw a ball of paper back at Royce. "And some come looking for me, knowing I can give them more pleasure than the two of you combined. They know I'm capable of dominating them without any help."

King threw several more balls of paper, his aim getting better. "Either one of us can master a woman. But women like having two cocks inside her, not a cock and a piece of rubber!"

Blade laughed. "When I'm with a woman, she gets so aroused, she doesn't care about things like that. I make her feel so good, she doesn't care about anything but release."

King threw another ball of paper, followed by yet another. Royce joined in, both aiming for Blade's head.

Blade retaliated, lobbing the balls of paper back, bawdy insults flying as fast as the paper. The insults had degenerated until their jibes had sunk to the level of high school boys, the hilarity culminating when Sebastian had walked through the door.

The usually stalwart butler had stood there gaping in amazement at his three employers antics, taking in the wadded balls of paper they'd thrown at each other and the way they laughed uproariously while insulting each other like teenagers.

Blade and his partners had laughed hysterically at the look on Sebastian's face before Blade stood, shaking his head, and chuckling as he headed for the kitchen, reminding them both to clean up the mess.

Two paper balls had hit him on the back of his head on his way out.

He couldn't remember ever laughing so hard, and he knew it was mostly due to the joy he felt having Kelly in his life.

Careful to be quiet, he opened the bedroom door and frowned.

Kelly lay curled into a tight fetal position with a pillow over her head, her hands fisted to hold it in place.

How could anyone sleep that way? And why would she sleep in such a defensive position?

Placing the tray on a side table, he moved silently to the bed. With the intention of easing her awake, he sat on the bed, shocked to the core at her reaction.

Kelly jerked awake with a scream, her arms flailing as she scrambled for the far side of the bed. Blade watched her wrestle with the covers when her legs tangled in them as she fought to kick out at him.

"Kelly, love, it's me." He kept his tone soft and soothing as she fought.

He stayed still, not wanting to frighten her further and kept speaking to her in the same low voice, praying it would get through to her.

"It's me, Kelly. Calm down, love. It's Blade, honey. You're all right. Nobody's going to hurt you."

With a last kick of the covers, she fell to the floor and quickly scrambled to her feet, her hands held out in front of her as though warding off an attack.

The terror in her eyes shook him to his soul. He hadn't seen fear in her eyes in a long time and he'd hoped to never see it again. But, what he'd seen before paled in comparison to what he saw now.

Careful to keep his fury hidden, he continued to speak to her reassuringly, immensely relieved when she became fully aware of her surroundings.

"You're all right, love. You're here with me. No one will ever hurt you again."

He stood and moved slowly to her, fighting to keep his voice low and steady as he approached her.

The tears on her face infuriated him even more. When he finally reached her and pulled her into his arms, he trembled almost as hard as she did.

Blade didn't allow the murderous rage he felt show on his face until he cradled her firmly against his chest.

Mortified, Kelly hid her face against Blade's chest. It had been a long time since she'd awakened from a deep sleep to find herself fighting for her life.

She should have known that sleeping with someone would eventually set it off. The only times she'd been touched as she slept had been when Simon caught her unawares and raped her.

With her head pressed to Blade's chest, she heard his heart race and could only imagine what he thought about her reaction.

Probably that he had hooked up with a crazy woman.

He caressed her back, his touch soothing her. Finally realizing how tightly she gripped him, wincing as she thought of how her nails had dug into his back, she loosened her hold.

He lifted her chin, gazing at her tenderly.

"Are you all right, love?"

She felt herself flush and nodded.

"I'm sorry, I …"

"Don't. Do not apologize for that. Ever."

His lips felt warm and soft, loving, as he kissed every inch of her face with slow deliberation.

By the time he reached her lips, she felt as if she floated, every trace of fear gone.

"I brought you breakfast."

Kelly noticed for the first time that Blade had already dressed. So, he hadn't been sleeping with her when she'd come awake like that. She frowned.

"You're dressed."

He tucked her back into the bed and brought the tray to settle over her lap. She pulled the sheet up to cover herself, tucking it beneath her arms, happy that he didn't comment on what had just happened.

"Yes, sleepyhead. I've been up for quite a while. I needed to take care of a few things before we go away."

"What do you have planned for me for our honeymoon?" She kept her voice deliberately teasing, so he would continue to ignore what had happened.

He leaned down, lifting her chin with a finger beneath it and dropping a hard kiss on her mouth. "If I told you, you wouldn't be surprised. You're just going to have to wait and see."

Kelly flushed in pleasure and deliberately lowered her gaze to the tray. He'd brought her coffee, orange juice, an assortment of sliced fresh fruit, toast, and an enormous omelet.

"I know I'm fat, but there's no way I'll be able to eat all this! I hope some of it's for you."

"Mmmm, it looks like I have to add yet another punishment to our honeymoon plans."

Kelly froze. "I was only, I mean…"

"I know what you meant. You've already been warned, though. You are lush and voluptuous. I thought I'd already made it clear how much I love your curves." He traced a finger over her shoulder and down to the curve of her breast.

"You did. I mean, you do. I just…"

"You just decided to insult what's mine. You've been warned about it before and chose to disregard my warning. A punishable offense. Now, eat your breakfast. I've already eaten. I didn't know what you would be in the mood for, or how hungry you'd be after last night, so I ordered a selection for you. Besides, you know how the staff loves to spoil you."

He poured coffee for both of them as he spoke, fixing hers the way she liked it automatically.

She took a bite of the omelet, humming in approval as the flavors of the vegetables and cheese burst against her tongue.

"This is delicious."

Blade smiled indulgently. "You can tell the chef how much you liked it. He's already making one of your favorites for dinner." He held up a hand before she could ask. "I can't tell you. He wants to surprise you."

Kelly smiled and took another bite.

"Did Simon attack you in your sleep?"

The sound of the fork clattering on the tray sounded loud in the room as Kelly hurriedly reached for her orange juice. Washing down the bite of omelet she'd almost choked on, she avoided Blade's eyes. "I don't want to talk about it."

"Incredible. You've earned two punishments and you haven't even finished your breakfast yet."

Kelly shivered involuntarily. She knew he wouldn't stop until he knew the truth. Lowering the glass of juice back to the tray, she folded her hands in her lap, her appetite forgotten. "I woke several times to him raping me. Sometimes he would hit me while I was still asleep."

Her frown deepened. In all the nights she'd slept next to Blade she'd never once woken in fear. She should never have been able to sleep with someone touching her. Her confusion must have shown on her face. Blade curved a palm over her cheek and forced her to meet his eyes.

"You sleep like a baby cuddled against me every night. This morning while I showered and dressed, you rolled onto my pillow and lay sprawled in abandon. When I came back with your breakfast, you slept in a tight little ball and held a pillow over your head."

Kelly felt her face grow warm. "I don't know what to say. I hope I don't disturb your sleep, cuddling against you like that."

Blade grinned. "Oh, you disturb me all right, but not in the way you're talking about. Having a warm, curvy, naked woman, one who responds to my every touch, sleeping and vulnerable in my bed is bound to give me ideas."

Kelly felt her nipples harden and clenched her thighs together as she wondered what sort of ideas Blade had had. Knowing him, they must have been really good ones. She hoped he'd act on them next time.

She couldn't believe that after all they'd done together, he could still make her blush. She fought to ignore it and resumed eating.

Kelly felt Blade's scrutiny as she picked at her breakfast. The cool mask slid over his features, hiding his thoughts.

When he began brushing the back of his fingers over her breast through the sheet, she gave up all pretense of eating. She looked down, unsurprised to see her nipples poking at the sheet.

"I was very worried when you woke frightened," he began.

Kelly lifted a hand to his cheek. "I'm sorry…"

"Mmm, three punishments. Be quiet and let me finish."

He waited until she nodded before speaking. "I was afraid that using that last plug in your bottom last night might have triggered some bad memories."

She opened her mouth to speak, but a sharp look from him had her snapping it shut again.

"It humbles me to realize just how much you do trust me. I didn't know how hard it would be for you to allow yourself to be vulnerable enough to sleep with me."

Kelly stared up into eyes that had darkened with emotion. She felt her own eyes sting and couldn't look away.

"I didn't think about it before," she whispered.

"I know, love. Subconsciously you trust me more than I could have ever hoped. You trust me enough to sleep curled against me, even to sleep peacefully while I'm still here. It wasn't until I left the room that you curled into a protective ball and put your guard up. You trust me enough to feel safe with me even in your sleep."

He leaned toward her and touched his lips to hers lingeringly. "I will never betray that trust, love. I'm honored, that after all you've been through, you would feel safe with me. I will never give you cause not to trust me."

"Oh, Blade," she sniffed. With her hands in his hair, she drew him back down again and felt him draw the sheet from her breasts.

"Even with the other women you touch?" she teased.

"Especially with them. I'm going to need all my energy to keep my wife satisfied."

When his hands covered her breasts, she automatically arched into his touch and heard the tray rattle.

"Enough." Blade pulled away with a grimace. "Finish your breakfast and go take your shower. You have a lot to do today and I have to go get some things together. I'm going to need several items on our honeymoon to effectively punish my wife."

Epilogue

Kelly came out of the sumptuous master bathroom of the house Blade had rented on the Gulf Coast. She walked into the bedroom wearing only the sheer white robe Blade had just given her, a cloud of vanilla wafting behind her.

She came to an abrupt halt as she took in the scene before her, her eyes widening in absolute shock and need.

Every erogenous zone in her body flared to life in an instant as she took in her husband's preparations for their wedding night.

Kelly gulped. *Uh oh.*

Blade stood next to the bed watching her, his arms folded over his bare chest, wearing black silk pajama pants and nothing else. The bed had been stripped of all coverings except a black silk sheet.

Candles burning all around the room provided the only light, casting eerie shadows that added to the look of supreme dominance on Blade's face.

Uh oh!

Kelly started to get the feeling that maybe, just maybe, she shouldn't have spent the past month daring Blade the way she had.

But, it had been such fun!

Their loving had sometimes been soft and slow, sometimes more demanding, but he hadn't punished her at all. She shivered remembering the many times his eyes promised retribution at every 'infraction.'

He'd kept his word, waiting for their honeymoon to exact his revenge and she learned more and more every day that Blade *always* kept his word. He'd told her as they'd pulled up to the house that he'd purposely picked one that didn't have any close neighbors, so no one but him could hear her screams.

Kelly gulped again when she took in the glitter in Blade's eyes and the large assortment of 'toys' he'd laid out on the chest at the foot of the bed.

Uh oh.

On it lay a large assortment of plugs, dildos, lube, paddles, and even a whip that had a lot of leather strips hanging from it. Glancing at the bed, she saw that cuffs had been attached to each of the four posts.

Every item she noticed drove her excitement higher, none more than the look on her husband's face and his beautiful lean muscular frame that now belonged to her.

"Hello, *wife.* You look beautiful."

"Thank you, darling. You look scrumptious."

She gestured toward the chest. "Does all that mean I'm in trouble?"

He grinned devilishly. "I would say after the way you've provoked me this past month that you're in a *lot* of trouble."

Kelly felt her bottom clench in response. "I'll be good," she promised, smiling.

"That's good to know," he said in amusement.

"So, all of this," Kelly waved her hand at the array of toys, "is really unnecessary."

She unconsciously played with her choker. When he only lifted a brow, looking at her in that way that always made her wet, she bit her lip to keep from smiling.

"Come here."

Kelly sauntered over to stand in front of him, lifting her face for his kiss. He obliged her.

"See how well you behave when I'm not flat on my back? Let's see if I can *persuade* you to want to be a good girl all the time."

He reached down and gripped the globes of her ass in his hands, his mouth at her ear. "I'm going to finally take this ass tonight, and when I do, you're really going to scream."

Kelly's breath caught as Blade picked her up and laid her face down on the bed, covering her body with his.

Feeling his hot length push between her parted thighs, she tried to move so it would rub against her slit. "Oh, Ahhh, Blade!" She tried to tilt her hips, needing to have him inside her.

"No, love." He bit her shoulder. "My cock isn't going in that tight pussy this time. This time you're going to give yourself to me in the ultimate act of submission."

His lips feathered across her ear. "Your husband and master is going to fuck your incredibly tight ass slow and deep."

"Oh God, Blade! I'll never be able to stand it!"

"Yes, love. You will." He lifted off of her and gripped her hips, raising them until her ass was now high in the air. "Keep those shoulders down. If you lift up, I'll punish you and then restrain you."

She'd been aroused since they walked into the house and every second her arousal grew. That dark cool tone he used now sent jolts of white hot need racing through her. She could feel the air on her drenched folds as he positioned her at the edge of the bed, her ass high and her knees spread wide.

Moaning in her throat, she tilted her hips upward, need overriding fear as her pussy and anus clenched. "Please, Blade. I need-"

A sharp lash landed and she jerked, crying out. The sensation of the leather strips of the whip caressing her bottom, had her all but crawling with need. "I know what you need." The heat spread deliciously as the leather stroked lightly over her slit.

Blade's hot hand caressed her bottom. "Nice and warm. The leather stroking your pussy is soaked." When she felt several more the light thrashes, she groaned, crying out her pleasure as she lifted into them.

"Blade, oh God! Please take me. I can't stand it."

"Have you forgotten that you don't make demands? I give the orders."

She couldn't help but rub her breasts against the sheet. The sensation of the silky sheet stroking her nipples had her close to coming already. She rocked her hips helplessly, silently begging him to end this torment. When a light strike of the whip hit her clit, she screamed.

"Blade, I'm coming. I can feel it come. It won't stop. It won't finish." Screaming her frustration, she rocked her hips harder. Little shivers of pleasure ran through her as her clit swelled, feeling at least twice its normal size. She didn't care what he did, she had to finish going over.

Reaching for her clit, she screamed when he caught her hand in his. "No! Let go! I have to come!"

She lifted up, only to have her shoulders pressed back down to the mattress as two fingers, covered with the cold lube surged into her anus.

"Ohhh! Ahhhhh! Yes! More!"

She bucked on his fingers as he held her down.

"You are the most undisciplined sub I have ever seen. I think it's time to show you who's in charge here."

Kelly froze when she felt his fingers slide out only to be replaced by the thick head of his cock. "Please, Blade. Fuck my ass. Please, take me!"

When the head began to push forward, chills ran down Kelly's spine. "Oh God! It's different! I don't think I can do this!"

"Yes, you can. You have no choice. No, relax that tight ass and let your husband inside."

Blade pushed forward and Kelly felt taken in a way she never could have imagined. This didn't tear her apart with pain the way Simon had. This didn't just feel vulnerable the way it did when Blade pushed the plug inside her.

This felt *submissive!*

She felt taken as never before, as if he owned her very soul as he stroked his thick heat deep inside her anus and stroked deliberately.

"See how nicely you're bent for me. I can take you as deep as I want as fast as I want for as long as I can last and you can do nothing but feel. Concentrate on the feel of it, love. Feel how much of yourself you're giving to me."

Too far gone already, Blade's words in that dark voice sent her over. Feeling every bump and ridge of his cock, she clenched on him tightly as she screamed her release. The burn in her bottom set off another orgasm as Blade continued to stroke into her. Her entire body shimmered with pleasure, spasms of release jerking her body uncontrollable. Her continued cries filled the room and she barely heard Blade's growls of pleasure.

His thrusts got hard and fast as he bit off curses. "You're too fucking tight, love. Come again for me."

"I can't!" Kelly cried, just as he surged deep and reached around to grip her clit.

This time, the pleasure became too intense, consuming her with its force. She heard Blade's growl of release as she tightened on him yet again and couldn't seem to loosen her hold. And just kept coming.

It took forever before she began to come down. Half asleep, she felt Blade move. He lifted off of her and she couldn't prevent a groan when he withdrew from her bottom as the thick head once again passed through the tight ring of muscle at her opening.

Absently aware of his lips on her shoulder before leaving the bed, she turned her head and watched him go into the bathroom. Closing her eyes, she must have dozed, because the next thing she knew, he got back into the bed beside her and pulled her close. When he handed her a glass of champagne, Kelly thanked him hoarsely

Still damp with sweat and breathing heavily, she groaned. "Oh, my God! The plugs didn't feel like that."

Blade chuckled. "They were only supposed to stretch you, love. It's not the same."

"I'll say." Kelly sipped again. "I want a shower."

"We'll take one together in a minute." He took her now empty glass and put it with his on the nightstand.

"I love you, Kelly. I want to have a family with you, grow old with you."

Tears pricked Kelly's eyes. "Oh, Blade. I love you so much. Can we really have babies?"

"Absolutely. When we get home, I'm going to talk to Boone and Chase about building a house for us. Living at the club is all right for now, but it's not a place to raise children."

Kelly sighed when he nuzzled her neck. "Blade?"

"Hmm?"

"I'm not going to be the kind of wife who obeys her husband. You've made me feel free. I like it too much to go back."

Blade's laugh caught her off guard. When he rolled away, laughing even harder, she frowned.

"I mean it, Blade."

When this only set him off again, Kelly glared at him and stomped off to take a shower. If he wanted to laugh at her, he'd have to do it alone.

When Blade joined her in the shower, he still smiled as he folded her in his arms. "Oh, love. You are such a delight. I absolutely adore you."

Kelly's insides clenched when he lowered his mouth to hers. He took her lips, eating at them as he pressed her back against the tile. Raising his head, he lifted her and sucked a nipple into his mouth.

"Blade!"

"Yes, love?" He raised his head and smiled at the woman who'd stolen his heart, his blood heating when her eyes darkened.

"You laughed at me!"

"No, love. I laughed because I knew that once you got your confidence back you'd be a force to reckon with." He bit a nipple. "And you are."

He moved to her other breast. "You challenge me on every level and I can't imagine not having you in my life."

She frowned in confusion. "Then it's okay when I disobey you?"

"No. When you disobey me, you're going to be punished." He lowered her slowly to the shower floor, sliding her wet body down the length of his, enjoying the way she felt against him.

"But, I'm going to disobey you sometimes. You're too strict!" She stomped her foot on the shower floor.

God, he adored her!

He turned her around to face the wall and leaned down to bite her earlobe. "Yes, love, I know." His cock hardened even more when he felt her shiver. "I'm going to have to spend the rest of my life taming you."

Kelly groaned when he parted the cheeks of her bottom and pressed his cock against her puckered opening.

"Tame me?" She tried to sound indignant, but when Blade began to press his length inside her tight opening, it came out breathless. "Oh God!"

"Yes, love." His fingers reached around and she felt them press into her pussy, now penetrating her in both openings.

He began to stroke into her and she fought to breathe.

"I won't let you tame me," she whimpered at the incredible fullness.

His mouth closed over the sensitive spot on her neck and bit gently, making her cry out in bliss.

"Yes, love. I know," he crooned.

Then her senses soared, as she heard nothing but the sounds of their lovemaking for a long time.

THE END

www.SirenPublishing.com/LeahBrooke

ABOUT THE AUTHOR

Leah Brooke has always loved to read and is addicted to happily ever afters. A bit of a daydreamer, for years she's written stories for her own amusement.

At her mother's encouragement, she decided to send one in.

Her first manuscript was born.

Since then, she spends most of her time working on the happily ever afters that keep racing through her mind.

Siren Publishing, Inc.
www.SirenPublishing.com

Breinigsville, PA USA
15 July 2010
241870BV00003B/66/P